MRS B RIDES AGAIN

Debbie Hewson

Mrs B began as a short story. Since then, she has found her annoying, nosey, accurate way into my life and the lives of those who have read her adventures and are hungry for more. This is her second book of stories. She has been fun and I wish her a safe journey, in her comfortable shoes, wearing a very smart hat, aboard her bicycle or striding through the country lanes. She is, I hope you will agree, rather wonderful.

My family and friends are a very patient group of people who have been very supportive of my being distracted, or of my disappearing to write, and I thank them all. They are the very best part of me, and always will be.

Love

Debbie x

1.

Mrs B seeks advice

"Mrs B? Are you quite well?" The Reverend Chambers walked through the multicoloured light filtered through the stained glass.

"I thought I was, but I am completely uncertain now. I wonder if I might ask for some advice?" She shifted her weight on the hard wood of the pew.

"Of course. My goodness, it is usually the other way around with you and me, but I would be delighted to help if I can." He sat in the pew in front of hers, and waited for her to tell him the problem.

"I know that I can trust that what I tell you is in confidence. To be truthful, I am not certain that I have even allowed myself to think about this before. Saying it out loud is somewhat challenging." She stretched her lips into a smile which felt entirely unnatural.

"If it helps, I am slightly wrongfooted in this situation, too." He leaned back into the seat. "Since I have come to this village, you have been such a strong support. I am nervous as to my ability to help, but I hope that I can."

"My husband was a good, honest man. He loved me. I know that he did. He went to war with a promise to me on his lips." A tear slipped unheeded down her cheek. "I thought I loved him, too. I did love him." She took a breath to steady herself. "I met Will Hunton long before I met my husband. But we were very young. When he came back, I realised that what I felt for my husband was nothing like love. It was polite, kind, gentle. Nothing like love. I would have gone on for a whole life with him, thinking I was loving, but walking when I should have been running. I know that now."

"I am so glad for you. That your husband loved you, and that you found love again." His smile told her he had understood nothing that she had told him.

"My mistake. I should have explained what I meant. I am eaten alive with the guilt. I have betrayed the man who loved me. The good, honest kind man who tried to give me a life, but gave up his on a beach in France. I did not deserve his love." She pulled a small handkerchief from her sleeve and dabbed at her eyes and nose.

"If I may?" He raised an eyebrow. "I can only speak as a man who loves his wife. If anything were to happen to me and she met someone who made her happy or, better still, happier than I did, then I would be glad for her. I would want her to be with that person." His voice shook a little. "Of course. I hope it doesn't happen." He rolled his lips over each other.

"Do you think he knows?" Mrs B struggled with the words. "Does he know that I have betrayed him?"

"You have not. Til death us do part. That was the promise. You have honoured his memory and his love. Forgive yourself. Nothing to forgive." He reached for her hand. "You are the most generous person, with your time and with your support. Please, give some of that to yourself."

The light filtered through the dancing dust motes in the aisle; he watched them surround Mrs B as she squeezed his fingers and walked out into the sunlight.

2.

Mrs B cleans her home

"You waited?" She stepped in through the back door. "You waited for me?"

"I told you I would. Tommy told me a few weeks ago that I had to stick to two rules. Never lie to you, and always wipe my feet when I come into your house." He shrugged. "I'm sticking to the rules."

"So am I. There are things in my house and in my heart that need to be cleared away. Parts of my life, my regrets. They need to be put to bed before I can make a start on a new life. I have something to tell you." She gripped the back of a kitchen chair.

"Come and sit down we can talk about it." He pulled out another chair.

"No, I need to say it now, or I won't be able to. Please." He nodded. "I love you. I did when you kissed me, when we were children, and I do now. For the record, I always will. It will take me some time to sort out how wretchedly guilty I feel about my husband." She pulled out the chair and slid down onto the seat. "I need a cup of tea." She rested her chin on her hand.

"Am I allowed to make tea in your kitchen?" He stumbled over the words.

"Oh, well, yes. I think you are. For heaven's sake, do not tell Maisie." A giggle slipped from her.

He emptied the kettle and filled it from the cold tap. "How am I doing so far?" She nodded. She watched him closely while he fetched the tea caddy and waited for the kettle to boil. He warmed the pot and spooned tea leaves in, then quickly poured the boiling water from the kettle.

"Perfect." He brought the cups and saucers to the table and placed the milk jug and sugar bowl between them. "Thank you." She poured the tea into the cup and added milk. Her first sip brought a smile to her lips. "Very good." She reached across the table and took his hand. "When everything is more organised in my head, and if you still want to, I would be very proud to be Mrs H." She raised her teacup in a toast, and Will met it with his. He stood up and lifted her from the chair, his arms wrapped tightly around her.

"I will wait. When you're ready, I will be waiting." She felt the words whispered against her neck, and the warmth of his body, and thought that she could stay exactly like that forever.

Reverend Chambers had been right. She could allow herself to be loved. There was no disrespect in what she was doing. Later, she would go through her house and decide what she had kept because she wanted it and what she kept because of her respect for her husband. There was hope bubbling through her that perhaps she could make a life with Will.

The sound of a tractor outside in the lane pulled them apart. Mrs Pendle was climbing down, with her little boy in her arms. His arms were waving about. Mrs B had always remarked on what a happy child he was. "Oh my, Mrs Pendle would have been surprised to have discovered us like that." She laughed.

"You would have been the talk of the village." Will laughed. "I will leave you to chat with Mrs Pendle. I'll leave this here for you." He slid the small box containing a ring onto the shelf. His lips touched her cheek, and he let himself out of the front door.

"Mrs B? Oh my, I don't know what to do about Grizelda. I need your advice if you have a spare minute?" Mrs Pendle bounced the smiling child on her hip.

"Of course. Let me make you a cup of tea." Mrs B poured out a cup from the pot, and forced herself to think about Mrs Pendle, and not Will's kiss.

3.

Mrs B and the Andersons

"Grizelda is, as you know, my prize-winning sow. She is the most productive of my pigs and I have only ever introduced her to one pig, and he has fathered all her piglets. When she was stolen, and you helped me to find her with your friend, she was due to meet with him again. You understand? But she was taken away. Nothing happened. Except it must have, because she's in farrow. It must have happened when she was with the Andersons." She ran her hand through her hair.

"I see. Is this a problem?" Mrs B's brow was furrowed in confusion. "Surely you can sell the piglets in the same way as usual."

"No. My piglets are sold to very discerning buyers. They know what they are buying, now I don't even know what I am selling." She sipped from the cup of tea. "I wondered if you might be able to find out from the Andersons who the father is. I have to be able to be honest with my customers. If one of them were to see a difference, I could lose everything. They trust me."

"I had no idea that people would be able to tell. I apologise for my ignorance." Mrs B offered a biscuit, but received a slight shake of the head. "Of course I will speak to the Andersons, but perhaps they would behave better if we gained the assistance of Mrs Newton. She was completely spectacular last time." Mrs B raised an eyebrow.

"Oh, yes, please. That would be a very good idea. Maisie's mum was a rather wonderful addition to the party." She stood up. "If you can give me her address, I'll send my husband to pick her up. I could go on the tractor, but it would take hours." Mrs B wrote the address on a piece of paper and watched Mrs Pendle climb back onto her tractor.

Mrs Newton would bring a different set of skills to bear on the situation. Mrs B checked her watch. There was time for her to call into the police station and catch up on their cleaning. By the time she was back, she fully expected to find Mrs Newton waiting for her.

4.

Mrs B goes looking for a pig

Mrs Newton climbed the hill towards the Anderson's farm. "This hill doesn't get any less steep, does it?" She huffed and puffed.

"That's for certain." Mrs B held out a hand and helped Mrs Newton the last few yards.

"Let me get my breath back, then I'll go and tell these two a few home truths." Mrs Newton leaned against the gate.

"Hold on, there are pigs in that barn. I can smell them." Mrs Pendle joined them at the gate.

Mrs Anderson walked out of the farmhouse into the yard. Mrs B pointed her out to Mrs Newton and watched her new friend pull herself up to her full height.

"I want a word with you." Mrs Newton bellowed across the yard. "I told you I would be back if anything happened to my friend's pig." She advanced towards Mrs Anderson.

"We have been nowhere near Mrs Pendle's farm. I promise you." Her voice shook over the words.

"You didn't need to, did you? She was already pregnant when we came and got her back. That pig is my friend's best breeder, and you've got her pregnant. I want to know which pig is the father. Right now." All the while she was speaking, Mrs Newton was crossing the yard towards Mrs Anderson, who stood and cowered.

"My husband thought if we could take the pig when she was ready for mating, we could get her in farrow and keep her under wraps until she had the piglets. It was our best hope to get started with a pig farm. We bought three sows with the last of our money and they turned out to be male." Her shoulders slumped.

"You're kidding. Who sold them to you?" Mrs Pendle stepped forwards.

"Mr Trot. We saw them in his yard, and they were sows, then he delivered these. We tried to get him to put it right, but he just laughed at us." She swiped away a tear.

"Show me the boys." Mrs Pendle suggested with a shrug. She followed Mrs Anderson into the barn.

Mrs Newton turned to Mrs B. "This Trot sounds like a piece of work."

"He has a reputation, but this is a dreadful thing to do. I know that Mr and Mrs Anderson behaved badly, stealing Mrs Pendle's Grizelda, but it seems it was desperation that made them do it." She turned to look towards the barn. Mrs Pendle was emerging.

"It seems that we have come to an agreement. Mrs Anderson has been defrauded. However, one of the boys in there is really rather wonderful. He is the father of Grizelda's piglets. I have offered that I will give the Andersons two of the female piglets, and the use of my boy, when they are old enough, and I will use their boy, to bring some fresh blood into my farm. It works for both of us, and they will have a pig farm up and running in less than a year." She turned to Mrs Anderson. "Better to work together than be fighting each other."

"Thank you. We came here for a fresh start. I can't tell you how much this means to me." She reached for Mrs Pendle's hands. "Thank you."

The three women walked back down the hill. There was silence between them. "I think Mr Trot needs a visit. He has always sailed a little too close to the wind, but this is theft. He has pushed too far this time." Mrs B shook her head. "What is Little Mellington coming to?"

"One of the boys he dumped on her is worth having. The other two, honestly, are only useful for sausages. I've explained to Mrs Anderson that she is feeding them for no good reason." Mrs Pendle shrugged.

"That's harsh." Mrs Newton's brows furrowed.

"Farming is harsh. I've spent years building

my farm. Every decision I make could put everything in danger. Mrs Anderson will need to learn really quickly. I'll help her, but I can't stop her from making mistakes." Mrs Pendle stopped at Mrs B's gate. "Thank you for helping today. Both of you."

Mrs B and Mrs Newton waved goodbye and went inside. "That man, Trot, he needs a lesson in manners."

"Yes, indeed, he does. I believe I know exactly the person who can teach him." Mrs B smiled. "Now then, how about a cup of tea?"

5.

Mrs B enlists some help

"That is outrageous behaviour, I agree, but I doubt that Mrs Anderson, from what you have told me, would be interested in giving evidence." Arnold held out his hands.

"Arnold, Mr Trot sold those people pigs and delivered completely different animals. That is fraud, surely. Or theft?" Mrs B rapped her frustration on the table.

"He will deny it, say that he delivered what was agreed." He shrugged. "I can't prove that it's untrue."

"What if he admits it?" Mrs B leaned her elbows on the table.

"Oh no! You are not going to go in and start digging about. Fred Trot is an unpleasant man. He has been violent in the past. This is not the same as analysing a crime after the event. You would be walking into his home." He laid his hand on hers.

"Is he worse than Mr Newton, or Mr McKinley?" She raised an eyebrow.

"I am not going to win this one, am I?" He had recognised the determination in her face.

"I very much doubt it." She laughed. "Come with me. If he's as much of a criminal as we think, you will be earning yourself some serious points with the higher ups." She raised an eyebrow.

"Fine. Come on, we may as well get it out of the way." He shook his head, and she followed him out of the house to his car.

Mr Trot's farm was a little outside the village. It was remote and the road that passed it saw very little traffic. It was the perfect place to be if you wanted to keep things hidden.

"He will talk more freely to me than to you, I suspect. I have known him for years, although not well." She watched him think about it, and keep driving.

"Fine, you go and talk to him. I will hang back and listen. Be careful though." He leaned against the wall of the barn, then regretted it, and brushed the dust from his jacket.

"Mr Trot? Mr Trot?" The man who turned towards her had aged a good deal since the last time she had seen him. "Mr Trot? I hope you remember me? You knew my husband, Herbert Blandford?"

"I remember him. He died in the war. Good man, he was." He stuck his hands in his pockets.

"Yes, he was. I hoped that you might be able to help me. My husband always said that you were a decent person. I have heard something that worried me recently, and I wanted to check with you if it could be sorted out." She smiled her most innocent smile at him.

"Herbert said that?" His brow furrowed while she nodded. "I will do what I can to help." His expression was one of surprise. Perhaps nobody had described him as decent before.

"Wonderful. Can you tell me what happened to Mr and Mrs Anderson's sows? It seems that when they were delivered, they had turned into boys." She kept eye contact with him and waited while he thought about it.

"No. That Anderson is a liar. He never said he wanted sows. Just pigs." His voice was low, he muttered into his chest.

"You showed them sows, though?" He nodded. "You knew that they were starting a pig farm, and you're a clever man, you knew that they needed sows for breeding." She nodded, and he nodded along with her. "I suppose you thought it was a joke. But it will bankrupt them. You are a decent man. You could help them. They only want to swap two of the three boys."

"No. Deal's a deal. They're not children." He kicked a stone across the yard.

"They are as far as farming is concerned. You

know they have only just started out. You and I have a responsibility to newcomers to the village. We have been lucky enough to live here our whole lives. Have we not?" Mrs B took a step towards him.

"I did not cheat them. You know that I am a decent man. I let them be the fools they are. That's all." He laughed, but it died on his lips when he saw her expression.

"You know that my nephew is a police officer. I have no wish to waste his time coming down here and tramping all through your farm. He's so busy these days." She raised an eyebrow and waited.

"Fine. I will swap them one sow." He snarled. "Tell them to collect her this week."

"A breeding female. Not too old or too young. A productive sow. If you please." He kicked his boot across the stones again. "Mr Trot?"

"Alright." He barked the word at her.

"Wonderful. I will ask Mrs Pendle to check the sow over for me. She knows her pigs. We will be back tomorrow to collect and drop off the boy." She smiled. "Just as Herbert told me. You are a decent man." She checked her hat was on straight. "Good day to you, Mr Trot."

Arnold laughed all the way home. "Uncle Herbert never said he was a decent man."

"Arnold, nobody ever said that Fred Trot was a decent man." Mrs B laughed too.

6.

Mrs B and Mr McKinley

"Mrs B?" The man on her doorstep was very like her friend, but older, wider and looking furious.

"Mr McKinley. How lovely to see you again." She waited. Perhaps he had something to tell her.

"I wondered if you might spare me ten minutes. Tommy says you are very good at giving advice." He smiled, and she saw something of his son in his face.

"I was about to make a cup of tea. Come on in." She held the door open. He followed her through the house and took a seat at the kitchen table.

"My wife died when Tommy was too young to lose his mother. I should have helped the boy more, but I could barely breathe in and out without her. When he went to prison, I barely noticed. That is a terrible thing to say, but it's the truth." He ran his hands through his hair.

"He understood." She put the tea in front of him. "He is a loyal young man. To you, to Maisie. Maybe even to me." She offered milk and sugar. "You taught him that."

"He loves her. That much is clear. I know that you have already helped him. I'm grateful. Tony Newton and I have been in competition for so many years. My wife always talked me into stepping back from confrontation with Newton. She said there was space for both families. Look how right she was. Now Tommy is engaged to Maisie. Neither of them is interested in the business. The argument, feud, whatever it is, finishes with Tony Newton and me." He shook his head. "We could have been stronger together, but both of us were too stubborn, I suppose." He sipped from the cup. "Thank you for the tea."

"May I tell you something?" He nodded. "I have had reason to speak with Mr Newton quite regularly with regard to Maisie. The two of you are so similar. Both of you have made a life based on your own physical strength, on the determination to be in charge. Perhaps in another life you could have been friends. It's still possible, but it would take a great deal of work. Maybe tolerating each other would be a start. You have a wedding to attend, at the very least." She patted his arm.

"Tommy was right. He said that he arrived here with problems and before he had finished a cup of tea, whatever was worrying him was gone. Maisie and Tommy say you have some sort of magic tea. I laughed when they said it, but now I'm not so sure." He nodded to himself.

"Would you like a biscuit? If you are going to accuse me of using magic, you had better experience everything." She laughed and put the biscuit tin on the table.

"Oh my. Well, Tommy was not lying about these." He chewed and closed his eyes for a moment. "It seems that he lied about nothing at all. That's new. He told me that you said not to lie. Not what I told him. To be honest, I have spent most of his life telling him to lie and cheat. I made him keep the secrets." He smiled across the table at her. "You're good at this, aren't you?"

"Drinking tea and offering biscuits?" She laughed.

"Listening. This is the most I have talked to anyone since, well, I suppose, since Jeannie died. She was the one who looked after Tommy. Looked after me, too. She was like that." He pushed his face into a smile, which looked uncomfortable.

"People told me that the years would help when my husband died. They were right, and they were wrong. It eases. The shock and so on. The other things, they stay, and sometimes they pop up and remind you. I envy you Tommy. I was left alone with no children, and I am too old now. You have Tommy, and now Maisie too." She took a breath and leaned her elbows on the table. "You have a family and a future to build on."

He studied his hands. "I'm sorry about raising my hand to you. My Jeannie would have been furious with me." He huffed a laugh. "My mother would have tanned my backside. To raise my hand to a woman, she would have been ashamed of me." He hung his head. "I am ashamed of myself."

"No harm done. In fact, although I do not condone your actions, it clarified some things that I have been mulling over." She shook her head. "Have another biscuit."

"I cannot resist." He took one. "Tommy is lucky to have found you. Thank you." He took in a breath. "You would not discuss what we have talked about?"

"Perish the thought. I would never share a confidence. This kitchen is very similar to a confessional, the same rules apply." She laughed. "There is always tea in the pot here."

"And stitches in your needle?" He raised his eyes to meet hers. She kept her stare level. "He told me. You're a riddle, Mrs B."

"I may well be, Mr McKinley, but I remain Tommy and Maisie's friend." She interlocked her fingers. "I hope that we can keep them safe between us."

7.

Mrs B gives her answer

A full ten minutes had passed since she had walked into his street. Most of those she had spent looking at the house. What on earth was going on with her? She was being ridiculous. A shake of her head made her check if she had dislodged her hat, but it was still where she had placed it, carefully secured with a hatpin.

Five steps took her to the front door. Her hand raised to knock. It was another last chance to back out.

She lifted the small brass knocker and dropped it onto the metal plate below. The door almost flew off the hinges. "Thank goodness. I thought you were going to give up and go home." Will held out his hand and reached for hers. "Whatever you have come to tell me will be better than not hearing from you." He stepped back, taking her with him into the hallway.

"I need to talk to you." She held tightly to his hand, feeling the warmth and the strength there. "I need to tell you a little about why I had to come to terms with my past actions, before I could make a future in all good conscience."

"Whatever it is, you and I will take care of it." He led her to his living room. "I promise I will always be on your side. Whatever happens, I will be your friend. We will be able to trust each other to tell the truth."

She watched his face, which had grown so dear to her. He meant every word.

She told him the truth, her words faltering and stumbling. The belief system on which she has built her life had taken a severe blow. Her image of herself as a grieving widow, left alone by the death of a loving husband, was threatened by the truth that her feelings for her husband had been less than she had thought. Her feelings for Will had frightened her, throwing a shadow over the memories of her husband. She would always regret that her husband had marched off to war, knowing that he loved her more than she loved him. Their love had been polite and kind, but without passion. The fire that she felt with Will was new and fired feelings of guilt and huge regret.

He listened, his eyes fixed on hers, and his hands wrapped around hers. When she had talked herself out, he waited, in case there might be more to come, but she had nothing left to say.

"I had no idea that you were feeling so unhappy.

Would you rather stop seeing me? Would that help?" Will moved closer to her and put his arm around her shoulders. It felt so wonderful.

"I don't want to stop seeing you." She rested her head back onto his shoulder and breathed. It felt as though they had been sitting this way for years. She fitted so easily into the curve of his body. The warmth of him seeped into her and she relaxed into him.

"Thank goodness for that." He huffed a laugh. "I really hoped that you would say that."

"May I ask if we could take it slowly? I am not very sure of myself and I need to find a way to steady these feelings." She turned so that she could see his face.

"I will wait as long as it takes. I will always be here for you, however long you need will be fine." He reached down for a kiss.

"In that case, I would be proud to wear your ring, Will." He reached into his pocket and pulled out the box.

"All yours." He slipped the ring on to her finger. "And you, my love, are all mine."

8.

Mrs B and Mrs Pendle

"Thank you so much for coming to check this sow over for me." Mrs B had chosen to walk rather than accept a lift on Mrs Pendle's tractor. "I am no expert on pigs, that is for sure."

"It's not a problem. That's what we do for each other, isn't it? We help each other." She checked over her shoulder and backed the trailer into the farmyard. "Afternoon, Mr Trot. Mrs B asked me to pop up and pick up a sow from you. I have one of your boys in the trailer. He's a nice-looking pig. If I had the money at the moment, I would buy him from you." She threw a smile, but Mr Trot's expression remained surly. He watched her jump down from the tractor and pointed to the barn. "Great, is that where she is?" He nodded but made no other response. Mrs B followed them both into the gloom of the barn.

The smell of the pigs was heavy in the air. Mrs B's only experience of pig farms was Mrs Pendle's farm, which was kept clean. These animals were not as lucky. The barn was sectioned off. The pigs were wading through dirty straw and it had been a while since it had been changed. Mrs B caught Mrs Pendle's nose wrinkling.

Mr Trot pointed to a pig. Mrs Pendle reached out and ran her hand under the pig's chin. She scratched between the sow's ears. The pig snuffled against her hand. "Hello lovely." She cooed as she climbed over the makeshift gate. "Let's have a little look." Mrs Pendle ran her hands over the pig's back and sides, and down her legs. "Is she the only sow you have?"

"She's the only sow I'm giving away." He growled, leaning on the gate.

"She's a bit on the light side, could do with a few good dinners." Mrs Pendle patted the sow's flank.

"Are you happy to take this one for Mrs Anderson?" Mrs B waited for Mrs Pendle to think about it.

"Yes. She's a better bet than what she has." Mrs Pendle nodded.

Mrs Pendle used a board to steer the young male out of her trailer and into the barn, and to take the female out of the barn into the trailer. "Thank you, Mr Trot. He's a good boy. If you want to sell him, I'll have enough to buy him from you in a couple of months."

"I'll think about it." He looked no happier. He pushed the gate shut on the young male.

"Thank you, Mr Trot. You have been most

helpful." Mrs B stepped away from the barn.

"Thank you, Mrs B." Mr Trot's voice was a whisper. "I was grateful that you kept your word. You could have sent your nephew in to investigate me, anyway." He pushed his hat back from his brow.

"Perish the thought. I would never do such a thing." She caught the tightening around his eyes, the slight movement around his mouth. "Don't worry. All I wanted was to resolve this matter. I've told nobody anything about you or your business." Mrs B tapped her hand on the gate. "Take care of yourself, Mr Trot."

"I thought you were an interfering old busybody when you came in here the other day. But you are as decent as the day is long." He turned to look at her.

"You were entirely right." She quirked a smile. "I am an interfering old busybody." She walked out of the farmyard listening to him laughing behind her.

9.

Mrs B and Mrs Anderson

The knock at the back door surprised Mrs B. She was not expecting anyone. She left her breakfast at the table and waited for Marmalade to move out of the way before she could open the door. "Good morning, Mrs Anderson. Are you well?"

"I am very well, thank you. Better than I have any right to be. I will not take up much of your time, but I know I owe you a debt of gratitude. We were desperate, but that is no excuse for what we did." She hung her head.

"Mrs Anderson, please come in and have a cup of tea. I just made a pot." Mrs B opened the door a little wider and ushered Mrs Anderson in. "It has all worked out well in the end. Mr and Mrs Pendle are doing very well with their pigs, and you could do a great deal worse than to take their advice." She poured a cup from the teapot and pushed it across the table to Mrs Anderson.

"Your friend, Mrs Newton? Do you know her husband?" Mrs Anderson wrapped her hands around each other.

"I know him a little. Is there something that I should know?" Mrs B took a bite from her toast.

"I want to tell you this, but I have to know that what I tell you will go no further." The lines around her eyes creased. Perhaps she was unsure whether she could trust Mrs B.

"Perish the thought. It is entirely your decision whether you tell me or not, but whatever you tell me is between us." Mrs B took a sip of her tea.

"We had to move." Her voice shook. "My husband was accused of stealing something. He has a past, as all of us do. But you would have to have lost the use of your mind to steal from Anthony Newton." She shook her head. "My Ronald, he came home one night and told me to pack what I could carry. That was all we took." She reached for the cup of tea.

"Oh my, that must have been most distressing." Mrs B shook her head.

"The thing is. Mrs Newton was angry when she came to tell me to give the pig back to your friend. We have a shared history with her." Mrs Anderson took a breath. "The thing is, she was in love with my brother-in-law before Mr Newton came along. Andrew ran out on her when she got too clingy. It was less serious for him than for her, I think." Mrs Anderson ran her hands over her face. "Anthony Newton asked my Ronald over and over again whether his brother could have been their Maisie's father." She pushed her hair out of her face. "He always denied it, but we don't know, not for sure."

"That is a difficult predicament." Mrs B pushed her plate of toast away. "You think that Mrs Newton is angry with you because of the danger that her involvement with your husband's brother could place her in?"

"Not that one! She's tougher than her husband ever was." Mrs Anderson laughed at the expression that crossed Mrs B's face. "She's afraid for her daughter. Truth is, she may not be sure which of them is the father." She rested her hand on the table. "Thank you for listening. I feel better for having told someone."

"I am grateful that you trusted me." Mrs B reached across the table. "I will not share this information with anyone. I promise."

"Thank you. I can see why Mrs Pendle has such faith in you." Mrs Anderson patted Mrs B's hand. She stood and buttoned her coat. "Be careful around Mr and Mrs Newton. They aren't like normal people. There's a hardness in them both. It's something that could hurt a normal person." She nodded and let herself out of the door.

Mrs B stood up and watched her walk towards the gate. The weather had changed and a light drizzle was falling.

The only people that were in need of her

protection were Tommy and Maisie. She would not be telling anyone what she had learned from Mrs Anderson, but now that she knew that there was a possibility, she would need to watch the Newtons very carefully.

10.

Mrs B has a meeting

"Mrs B?" Mrs Lennet was waiting outside Mrs B's cottage when she arrived home.

"Mrs Lennet? How very lovely to see you. Have you time for a cup of tea?" She opened the back door and held it open for Mrs Lennet.

"Thank you, Mrs B." Mrs Lennet stood just inside the door. She shifted her weight from one foot to another.

"Mrs Lennet? Please come and sit down and tell me what I can do to help?" Mrs B filled the kettle and set it on the gas ring.

Mrs Lennet sat down and wrapped her hands around each other. "Mrs B. You have helped me and my family so many times. I wonder if you can work your magic again. I am not certain that it is even possible to solve this one." She ran her finger under her eye.

"Oh, my dear Mrs Lennet. I will do my best. Perhaps between us we can solve the puzzle?" Mrs B pushed herself up from the table when the kettle whistled.

"Yes. That is a good place to start. The thing is, my husband, as you may know, has decided to take things a little easier." She took a breath. "The doctor suggested that he had been overdoing things." She accepted the cup that Mrs B offered. "He will be at home a good deal more, and he thought he might take more interest in running the estate. Which is wonderful, of course." Her hand fluttered around the pearls that she wore at her neck. "I have always looked after that side of our life together. He is starting to suggest changes." She took a sip from her cup of tea.

"You feel as though he is taking over. You are worried that he will change the rules in what has been your domain." Mrs B nodded and sipped her tea. "Which he may wish to."

"I do. Yes, that's exactly it." Mrs Lennet closed her eyes. "I am being selfish and unkind, I know."

"No, just honest. Nothing wrong with that." Mrs B reached across for Mrs Lennet's hand. "Perhaps there is some middle ground to be found?"

"Oh yes, I would like that." Mrs Lennet sat a little straighter in the chair.

"If I were you, I would suggest that you go through the plans that you had for the year ahead, and see if he can add anything to them. It would be a starting point." Mrs B sat back and waited for her guest to think about the situation.

"That is a good idea. Thank you, Mrs B. I knew

that you would help." Mrs Lennet set her cup down on the saucer. "Now that you have settled my problem, perhaps you need to tell me your news."

"My news, Mrs Lennet?" Mrs B's brow furrowed in confusion.

Mrs Lennet reached across the table and took Mrs B's left hand in hers. She tapped her finger on the ring on Mrs B's finger. "This news."

"Oh. Yes. Well, that is news indeed." Mrs B lifted her hand to admire her ring. "I have been walking out with Will Hunton. He has asked me to marry him. It may not be immediately, but one day."

"Do you love him?" Mrs Lennet reached for Mrs B's hand.

"Yes. I do. More than I believed possible." A tear ran down her cheek.

"I am so pleased for you. You have helped so many people in this village. Certainly, in my family. You deserve all the happiness in the world." Mrs Lennet pulled a handkerchief from her handbag and dabbed her eyes. "I could not be happier for you. I hope that we will be invited. My family would love to celebrate with you." Her fingers squeezed Mrs B's hand.

"Will you talk to your husband?" Mrs B tipped her head to one side.

"So long as he agrees not to keep pigs. He has been talking about buying piglets. Talking to that dreadful man, Trot." She wrinkled her nose as though she could already smell the pigs.

"If you will take my advice, pigs may or may not be a good idea, but doing business with Mr Trot would be a mistake." Mrs B raised her teacup in a toast. Mrs Lennet clinked hers against it, and they sipped.

11.

Mrs B is invited to a wedding

The postman pushed the letters through the door, and they landed with a thump. Mrs B stooped to pick them up. The usual bills and a letter from a friend who had recently moved to a bungalow near the sea. Mrs B carried the envelopes through to the kitchen and sat to read the letter with her breakfast. It seemed that her friend was enjoying the sea air and walking on the promenade, and that made her glad. She would reply later in the day.

The bill from the gas board was next. It was no more than she expected, and she laid it on the table. A small envelope lay on the table, addressed by hand. She lifted the flap and slipped the letter inside onto the table. She read the letter through twice, with her hand over her mouth.

This was bad, and good in so very many ways. She sat in the kitchen while her breakfast grew cold on the table. There was only one possible course of action.

She left Marmalade to finish his breakfast and

cycled down the lane. The door to the church was open, and she quickly found the Reverend Chambers. "Good morning, Reverend. I wonder if you might have a moment?"

"Yes, of course. I always have time for my friends." He beamed so happily at her she felt a little unkind that she would be bringing worries to him.

"I have received a letter from Tommy and Maisie. They tell me that they are planning to marry, and that you have agreed to perform the service." She sat heavily in the pew.

"Yes indeed, Tommy came to see me, before they went off and asked. I was delighted." He sat with her, perhaps picking up some of her worry.

"You know their fathers?" Mrs B raised an eyebrow.

"Only by reputation." He nodded. "Tommy explained that it had all been discussed with both families, and I was not to worry.

"I see. I hope I see. That is…." She trailed off. "Have they set a date?"

"Not yet. But it is to more of a blessing than a marriage, I believe." The reverend gentleman watched Mrs B thinking her way through the information.

"No reading of bans, then?" He shook his head. "They will be married already when they return?

Special licence perhaps? I think Maisie is too young for that. I shall have to find out. Many thanks. I must dash." She rushed towards the door before remembering where she was and turning to bow towards the altar.

The bus ride seemed to take longer than she had remembered, perhaps because she was anxious to arrive at her destination.

When Arnold opened the door, she had rarely been more delighted to see her nephew. "Arnold, please, can you help me?"

12.

Mrs B and the mad dash

"We have no time to waste. Please Arnold, can you drive a little faster?" Mrs B's fingers were wrapped so tightly around the handle of her handbag that she was leaving marks.

"Auntie. Please stop. I will get us there as quickly as I can, and telling me to get you there quicker every five minutes will not make a difference." He pointed to the sign which they passed. "Look, we will be there in ten miles."

"I just hope that we will be in time." She put her handbag on the floor next to her feet and concentrated on wrapping her hands around each other.

What on earth would she do if she was too late? For that matter, what would she do if they arrived with plenty of time? She had dragged Arnold hundreds of miles from home and two days of driving and she still had not yet formulated any kind of plan.

They crossed the border into Scotland, and Arnold followed the signposts to Gretna Green.

"Are you sure that they will be here?"

"I am not certain of anything at all, Arnold." She shook her head. "I only know that Maisie was performing at a theatre twelve miles away yesterday, and they asked Reverend Chambers to perform a blessing. They wrote to me telling me that they would be married. Maisie is too young to marry under a special licence. This was the only place that made sense. I could be wrong. In some ways, I hope that I am."

The village was smaller than she had expected. The church was tiny. Arnold parked the car and, with more than a little trepidation, Mrs B pushed open the church door. The place appeared to be empty. She slid into a highly polished pew. It occurred to her that it was not so very different from the church she polished in Little Mellington. The smell of polish and freshly cut flowers hung heavily in the air. She breathed deeply, glad of the familiarity.

"Mrs B?" Tommy stood in the aisle. "What are you doing here?"

"Tommy? You said that you were getting married. Reverend Chambers said you were coming to him for a blessing. I came to ask you please to reconsider. Give your families time to come to terms with the life that you are planning." She reached for his hands and held them tightly.

"Well. That's a lovely idea. It's a little bit late, though." Tommy lifted her to her feet and wrapped his arms around her. "I am so glad that you are here to share our special time."

"I am too late." She stood back from his embrace.

"Mr McKinley?" The vicar cleared his throat. "I am so pleased that your family managed to attend."

Arnold turned at the sound of the door opening. Mrs B followed his gaze. "Oh Maisie, you look beautiful." Mrs B reached for the young woman in the doorway. "Lovely as you are, and as romantic as this is, please wait for your father and Tommy's father to accept the situation." She held tightly to Maisie's hands.

"They won't accept it. We just need to get on with our lives. I love Tommy and he loves me." She shrugged. "They're making it too complicated."

"May I ask you to at least telephone your father, and have Tommy do the same, before you make your promises to the man who loves you. Your father loves you, too." She stepped away from Maisie, who looked every inch the perfect bride. Her gown was floor length white silk. Mrs B thought back to Arnold and Barbara's wedding. It had been the day that she had met Tommy McKinley. She had argued to make sure that the wedding had gone ahead on that day. Did she have the right to argue against a wedding?

"Tommy? Mrs B has asked us to telephone your dad and mine. To tell them what we are doing. What do you think?" Maisie waited.

"Mrs B gives good advice. I trust what she says." Tommy turned to the Vicar. "It seems that we need to find a telephone."

13.

Mrs B and the telephone call

"Excuse me?" Mrs B made her way down the aisle towards the vicar. "Please help us reverend." The gentleman nodded his assent, his bushy moustache wobbling alarmingly. "The bride and groom need to speak to their respective families. I wonder, where is the nearest telephone?"

"Ah, I can assist, madam. There is one in the police station next door." He smiled. "Or the telephone box in the street."

"Wonderful. Thank you." She patted his hand. "They will be back very shortly. You know how complicated families can be?" She rushed back to Maisie and Tommy. "There are two telephones, one in the police station, and there is a public telephone box in the street. I think neither of your fathers would appreciate a call from the police station." She gently led them both to the church door. "You are being very sensible. You have a whole life ahead of you, and your fathers will both be part of that."

Maisie bent to the floor and scooped the skirt of

her dress over an arm. "Come on then, let's get on with it." She huffed a sigh. "I know that you're right, Mrs B, but that doesn't mean I like it."

"I presume there is a telephone at the Royal Oak. Is there a way to reach your father, Tommy?" Mrs B stood still outside the red telephone box. Tommy nodded. "Who would like to go first?"

Tommy turned to look at Maisie. "Up to you."

"You first." Maisie watched him with her eyes wide open in her face. "This is going to be really difficult."

"Fine. I'll start." He dialled the operator and gave the number. The door began to close and Maisie stopped it.

"No secrets, we agreed." She left her hand against the door. Tommy reached out to hold the door open, too.

"It's ringing." He waited. "Hello, Dad?" There was a pause. "I'm in Scotland. Maisie and I are about to get married." He laughed. "Yes, in Gretna Green." He listened. "I know that, but Mrs B worked out what we were doing and got here in time to make us phone you. She reminded us that we might love each other, but you loved me before I met Maisie, and I want you in our lives, part of our family." He listened again. "Yes. The biscuits are fairly special." He laughed again, raising an eyebrow at Mrs B. "Yes, that's a good idea. I'll ask. Stay there for a minute so

I can telephone back. Alright, thanks Dad." He replaced the receiver. "He took the news better than I thought. Actually, he has invited your dad to go over and listen on the phone. If Mrs B will tell them what is happening, it will be like them being here." Tommy stepped out of the telephone box and held the door open for Maisie. "Your turn. Shall I hold your beautiful dress?"

"Yes please. This floor looks grubby." She passed the folds of fabric to him, giggling as she tried to reach the telephone receiver. She dialled the operator and gave the number, pushing coins into the slot. "I need to speak to my dad. It's Maisie Newton." There was a pause before she raised her eyebrows to signal that he was there. "Dad? It's me. I'm in Scotland. I'm ringing you because Mrs B made me. To be honest, I didn't want to. I'm marrying Tommy, my choice. He wanted to wait." There was shouting on the other end. "I know you are upset. But please just listen. We wrote to Mrs B, and I thought we had been really clever. But she worked out what we were doing and got here before the wedding. She made us telephone you; because she said you love me, and Tommy's dad loves him. Being married is about making a family. I want you to be part of ours. I love you, dad." She waited, listening. "Tommy's dad has invited you to his, and Mrs B will tell you what is happening, so it's like you're here. If you want to. Can you pick up Mum on the way?" There was a pause. "Yes. Probably. We are having a church service when we get back. A blessing. I'd like it if you would give me away, properly, and I'd like Mum to get a new hat." She swiped a tear away. "Half an hour. Fine. We will let him know you're on your way." She put the receiver back into the cradle. "He's on his way to your dad's place. He's taking a bottle with him and picking up my mum." Tommy's relief was apparent. With the air of a man who has a full half hour to wait, he leaned back against the railings.

"I thought for sure he would not forgive me for this." He let out a long breath. "I had better let my dad know to expect him."

Back in the church, the vicar was relieved that he would be able to carry out the service. Arnold agreed to be the go between. They explained the situation to the vicar, who laughed long and loud at the idea, but agreed that it would be the best they could do.

Over the next ten minutes, Arnold ran in and out of the church, shouting the progress of the wedding inside. Mrs B relayed every word that he said over the telephone to Mr Newton and Mr McKinley, who were sharing a room, a telephone and a bottle of whiskey.

"Thank you, Mrs B." Mr Newton sounded genuinely grateful on the telephone. She heard the clink of glasses and imagined that the two fathers had found something that they both wanted to celebrate.

"Mrs B? I am very unhappy that my daughter has done this. Worse than that, I have had to sit here with two men I would generally avoid like the plague." Mrs Newton's voice was harsh and Mrs B listened to her pull hard on her cigarette.

"You have wonderful children and you have something else in common." She heard their surprise. "You are part of a bigger family now, one that will blossom and grow, if you're lucky."

"You made them telephone us. Thank you for that. I am grateful." There was a noise in the background. "We are grateful. We will be looking forward to the blessing and actually seeing them take their vows in church." Mr McKinley's voice sounded different. Perhaps he had been affected by the wedding, or the whiskey, or a combination of the two. "Perhaps, can I ask one favour?"

"If it is something that is in my gift." She held the telephone receiver and waited.

"Can you make some of those biscuits for the reception? They would be sure to set the kids off on the right foot." He laughed, and in the background, she heard Mr Newton laughing too.

"Yes, of course. I will make them with pleasure." She smiled and said goodbye. The two men had been at loggerheads for years, and Mr and Mrs

Newton were clearly furious with each other, yet here they were raising a glass to being family. Human beings never failed to surprise her. They could be better, stronger, and more worthwhile than anyone could imagine.

At the door of the church, Tommy and Maisie were smiling widely. "Congratulations, Mr and Mrs McKinley." Mrs B reached to hug all the way around both of them. "I am so very proud of you both."

14.

Mrs B explains

"You have been to Scotland?" Will was clearly unhappy. She watched his expression turn from confusion to annoyance.

"I explained. I had a letter from Tommy and Maisie, and I thought I might be right. Of course, I was not entirely certain." She stood by the cooker and waited for the kettle to boil. "When I arrived, and it was only just in time, I was able to ask them to telephone their fathers. I think it was worth the journey." She watched him carefully. "Are you upset that I went?"

"You asked Arnold to take you. It never occurred to you to ask me." Of course, he was right. She bit down on her bottom lip.

"Yes. You're right." She sat heavily on a kitchen chair. "I should have asked you. I was stupid of me."

"Not stupid. It just shows that you don't think of me that way. You go to Arnold for help. What do you think of me for?" He looked straight into her face and held the stare.

"I'm sorry, Will. It was a thoughtless thing to do. I have been in the habit of going to Arnold. Of course, I was worried when I received the letter, and more so when I found out that they had booked a blessing with Reverend Chambers. I was wrong." She dipped her head.

The silence hung between them. She closed her eyes. Was this the stupid, thoughtless thing that would end the fairytale that she had been living in with Will?

"No." Will laid his hands flat on the table. "I did not mean that."

"You did, and you were right." She kept her eyes on the table.

"I am only going to say this once." He reached across the table. "You and I are going to be together. We will be equal in every way. I have no idea who told you that you owed me this abject apology; hanging your head in shame." He took her hands in his. "It is me who should apologise. You did not come to me because I have not made myself available to you as Arnold has. From now on, I will." He waited for her head to lift until her eyes were level with his. "Agreed?"

She swallowed, searching his face to be sure that he was being honest with her. "Agreed."

"We tell each other the truth and we take responsibility for what we have done or not done. Neither of us are children." He pulled a handkerchief from his pocket and passed it to her. "No need for tears or apologies. We are beyond that, my love." He wrapped his arms around her and held tight.

15.

Mrs B prepares for a celebration

The knock on her front door was unexpected. Most of her friends arrived by the back door, directly into her kitchen. Her surprise when she discovered Mr Newton and Mr McKinley on her doorstep sent her eyebrows shooting up towards her hairline.

"Mr Newton, Mr McKinley, please, come in." She opened the door, and they filled the small hallway. "Please, go through to the living room."

"May we go into the kitchen?" Mr McKinley turned to her. "It feels more comfortable." She shrugged.

She offered tea and placed biscuits on the plate. "How can I help?"

"We have discovered a few things over the last few days. Things that we would not have found out if you had not pushed our children to let us know about the wedding." Mr Newton looked across the table at Mr McKinley, who nodded back. "We have more in common than we have to divide us." He huffed a breath. "What we do not have, either of us, is a wife." Mrs B's brows pushed together.

"What we are trying to say is that neither of us has any idea what is needed to arrange a wedding. We are asking for your help." Mr McKinley offered a smile. "All we want is for them to have a wedding that they can look back on with happy memories. We will make sure that there is no fighting or arguing between the men who work for us. Beyond that, we will pay the bills and trust you to arrange everything." Mr Newton raised his hand to interrupt. "No. We have had this argument. Tradition says the bride's father pays, but we are splitting the costs. No more arguments." Mr Newton dropped his hand, and although his teeth ground together, he kept quiet.

"Well, I am so very pleased. It seems that you have found the common ground between you." She busied herself with the teapot and placed cups in front of each of them.

"Am I to understand that congratulations are in order?" Mr McKinley pointed to the ring on her finger.

Mrs B considered the situation. She would have to tell people, but she had not thought about that yet. "Yes. I am engaged to be married. To Will Hunton." She picked up her tea and sipped. It seemed strange to say it out loud.

"Well, I never." Mr Newton slapped his hand on the table. "I would not have thought that Will had it in him." He caught the frosty look that Mrs B sent his way. "I hope that you will be very happy. Perhaps you might investigate together, now that Tommy is busy looking after Maisie."

"One never knows what might happen, I suppose." Mrs B considered the future that she had imagined, and the future that she now saw as becoming reality. She would not have thought it possible just a few months before. "Now then, I shall fetch some paper and we will need to start planning this wedding." The first item on her list would be how to explain the situation to Maisie's mother.

16.

Mrs B enlists a team

"Barbara? I need your help." Mrs B hugged Barbara tightly. "We need to organise a wedding. You are tremendously resourceful and I am truly in need of your help."

"Auntie. How lovely. Yes, please. I love weddings!" Barbara passed Jennifer to Mrs B for a cuddle. "Is this anything to do with you and Will?"

"Oh, love, not for a while. This is for Maisie and Tommy." Mrs B propped Jennifer on her hip and smoothed her hair. "Would you like to go to a wedding, little Jennifer?" The little girl laughed and clapped her hands. "I suspect that is a yes."

"What do you need me to do?" Barbara sat down at the kitchen table and pulled out a pad and a pencil.

"We need to organise flowers, food, guests and music for the service and the reception. Also, invitations, I suppose." Mrs B leaned on the table. "All we have is the good news that Reverend Chambers has agreed to perform the blessing."

"Well, there's a start at least." Barbara started her list. "Have they given you any idea about what they want?"

"None at all. Their fathers arrived at my house and asked me to arrange the wedding." Mrs B lifted her shoulders.

"Fine. Let's choose the flowers, I think Maisie will have strong opinions about the music. We need a guest list from the families and food we can organise once we know how many to expect." Barbara made notes on her pad.

"I knew you were the right person to ask. I have written to Mrs Newton to ask her if I might visit her to ask for her preferences. I suspect that she will be unhappy that she is not organising the whole thing. There may be some ruffled feathers which need smoothing. Perhaps we need to include her earlier rather than later." Mrs B jiggled Jennifer on her knee.

"Now that, is a good idea." Barbara tapped the table with her hand. "Do you know what is another one? Let's make a cup of tea." Barbara patted Mrs B's hand and went to fill the kettle.

"Perhaps we should ask a few of the ladies from the village to help. What do you think?" Mrs B accepted the cup of tea and thought a little longer.

"Good idea. More hands would make light work of the whole thing. It will be fun, too." Barbara turned to a fresh page and began a new list.

"Mrs Appleby and Mrs Chambers are a whizz with the flower arrangements. We should ask them." Mrs B tapped her hand on the table. "Nobody is better than Mrs Gartree for decorations. If the weather is kind, we might have some of the celebrations outside."

"I liked Mrs Gartree. Nice lady." Barbara tapped the pencils on the table. "Will there be bridesmaids, a best man?"

"Heavens. I know less than I thought. I will ask for all this information. Thank you, Barbara." They raised their cups in a toast and clinked.

17.

Mrs B makes a correction

The walk up to the Manor was a pleasant one when the weather was good. However, the clouds were threatening rain and Mrs B hurried to arrive before the heavy shower that was imminent and would drench her.

The door was answered by a stiff-necked butler, who relaxed when he recognised Mrs B, and invited her inside as the first drops of rain fell.

"My goodness, I am so glad that I beat the rain." She smiled widely at him, unbuttoning her coat. "I have an appointment to see Mrs Lennet."

"Yes, of course. You are expected. Please come this way." She followed the man who walked, she thought, with a military gait.

"Mrs B? I am so pleased to see you. Do come in. You are, as ever, exactly on time. The tea is just ready for us. I hope that you will join me for a cup?" Mrs B had never that she could recall, turned down a cup of tea. After the quick march up the hill, it would be welcome. "Now, what was it that you wanted to discuss?"

"Mrs Lennet. I wonder if I may ask what you plan to do with the fields nearest to the village. They have always had sheep on them to my memory, but I passed by the other day and I see that they have been ploughed up. Forgive my question. There is a purpose." Mrs B gratefully accepted the cup of tea, and took a sip.

"Ah yes, you will recall that my husband had decided to take more interest in the estate. We discussed the whole thing, and he did have some useful ideas. You were right about that." She nodded her thanks for Mrs B's previous advice. "He suggested that we plant potatoes in those two fields. We have now ploughed up the ground, and the soil is not as good as we had hoped. The plans are therefore on hold until we can improve it." Mrs Lennet's brows pushed together. "Why were you asking?"

"I have a question, or perhaps a proposition." Mrs B shook her head, annoyed at her own search for the correct word. "Procrastination is the thief of time. I apologise, Mrs Lennet." She shared a smile with her hostess. "I have, I believe, been unfair to Mr Trot. Perhaps I judged him a little too harshly. In any case, I feel that I have been uncharitable, and that rankles with me. When we last spoke, I advised you against doing business with him, and that was mean of me. I did have an idea which might benefit both of you, and his pigs, if you were agreeable."

"That sounds like a very good idea. Please tell me what it would involve?" Mrs Lennet sat forward to listen.

"Mr Trot keeps pigs. Their pens are not as clean as they could be. I wonder if you might gain some improvement in your soil if Mr Trot were to deliver and spread the contents of the pig pens on your fields and that might be worth a small fee?" She watched Mrs Lennet think about the idea. "Once the frost comes, you could have the fields ploughed again and ready for planting by spring." Mrs B sat back and sipped her tea.

"His pigs would then be regularly given fresh bedding, and we would have fertile land. Mrs B, I think you may have discovered the best plan possible." Mrs Lennet set her cup down on the table. "I would be a little nervous to deal with him myself. Would you perhaps be prepared to speak to him on my behalf?"

"It might be better coming from Mr Lennet? Man to man and all that rot." Mrs B sat back on the small sofa. She had not realised how worried she had been about asking Mrs Lennet until it was over.

"You are a wonder, Mrs B. You have solved the problem for all of us in one go. Thank you." She picked up her cup again. "I think we should celebrate with a piece of cake, don't you?"

18.

Mrs B receives a surprise invitation

The postman was right on time. Marmalade ran towards the front door to see what had landed there. Mrs B followed him and collected the letters.

"What beautiful handwriting Marmalade. I must remember that for Tommy and Maisie's invitations." She showed the envelope to her cat, who was less interested than she had hoped.

Mrs B shook her head and carried the post through to the kitchen, where her breakfast was waiting. The beautiful envelope held a handwritten card in the same hand. "Please allow me the great privilege of escorting you to dinner. Fish and chips tonight? I will pick you up at seven" It was signed Will, with a flourish. She held the card between her finger and thumb. It was a beautiful and kind thought. A breath in and out, filled with gratitude for having Will in her life, brought a smile to her lips.

The day began with a visit to Mrs Chambers. Her house was a mess, with toys and baby clothes all over the living room. Mrs B could not determine which were clean and which dirty. She shrugged and filled the sink with hot water and soap. The day was warm, and a breeze lifted the freshly washed clothes. Mrs B left them to dry while she set the rest of the house straight.

When the clothes were ironed and piled in the basket on the kitchen table, Mrs B climbed onto her bicycle. She considered, as she rode, why Will might send her a handwritten invitation rather than just come to the house and suggest fish and chips. It seemed a grand gesture over something so simple.

The police station took less than an hour to clean, and rather than stopping by the canteen, she waved to Kathleen through the window and cycled home.

Will knocked on the door at exactly seven. "Hello. That invitation was beautiful. I am so touched that you went to so much trouble." She reached up to kiss his cheek.

"I wanted to tell you something." He produced a paper bag which he passed to her. It was warm.

"You picked up the fish and chips? How lovely. Come through, I will fetch some plates." She opened the bag and unwrapped the fish and chips inside. The steam which rose from the food carried the hot scent of vinegar as she laid out the battered cod and hot chips.

Mrs B turned to carry the plates through to the dining room and found that Will was sitting at the kitchen table. "I wanted to tell you something, and I thought that fish and chips might be the way to do it." He waited until she had sat down before he continued. "I love you. I am not an honoured guest. We don't have to eat in the dining room." He tapped his finger on the plate. "Or eat off your best plates." He popped a chip into his mouth and reached across to hold her hand. "I sent you a fancy invitation to a very ordinary meal because you make the most run-of-the-mill things wonderful. I could eat a sandwich, or drink a glass of water with you, and it would be better than the finest food in the world. Do you understand?" He wrapped his fingers around hers. "I love you. This is not a game. You are my life. From here on, I have no life unless it is with you. I have no heart unless you share yours with me."

Mrs B pulled a handkerchief from her sleeve and dabbed at her eyes. In two steps, she had rounded the kitchen table. Her lips met his. "Will, you have my promise, and my heart. I thought that you knew that."

"I do now." His smile lit up his face. "Your chips will get cold." He ran a finger down the side of her face.

"You're right. Can I come and sit with you on this side of the table? Let's meet whatever is coming together, rather than on opposite sides, shall we?" She pushed her plate across and moved her chair around so that they sat next to each other.

"Good idea. I like it much better this way." They shared a smile and Mrs B speared a chip with her fork.

"Lovely dinner. Thank you. My turn tomorrow night?" He turned toward her just in time to see the smile cross her lips.

19.

Mrs B and Mrs Newton

"Good morning, Mrs Newton. I wonder if you could spare me five minutes?" Mrs B stood patiently on the doorstep.

"Of course. Come on in." Mrs Newton led the way to the kitchen.

"I am in a tricky situation, and I wondered if you might be prepared to help me." Mrs B accepted the offered chair.

"Oh? What can I do to help you?" Mrs Newton busied herself putting the kettle on.

"I had a visit from Mr Newton and Mr McKinley. They insist that I make the arrangements for Maisie and Tommy's blessing. That puts me in a difficult position because, by rights, it should be you who organises it." Mrs B smiled and accepted the cup of tea she was offered.

"That puts me in a tricky situation, not you. My daughter's wedding, and I am not allowed to be involved." The words were clipped short.

"That is why I'm here. I wanted to ask you for

your help. I couldn't do it alone if I wished to. But I have no wish to. Maisie needs her mum on her special day, and I need your help." Mrs B took a sip from her cup. "Delicious tea. Just what I needed after the ride over here on the bus." She folded her hands in her lap and waited for Mrs Newton's reaction.

"Now, why would you do that?" Mrs Newton's mouth pulled into a tight line.

"I think Maisie needs you. Mr Newton and Mr McKinley have told me that they don't know where to start with planning. I have helped with planning weddings before, but I suspect you would have different ideas. Between us, we might be able to give them a really rather marvellous day." Mrs Newton tapped her fingernails on the table. "Unless, of course, you would rather not?"

"You are a conniving, difficult, annoying woman." Mrs Newton's nostrils flared with temper. "Unfortunately, you are also extremely kind and generous. I very much would like to help you plan." She sipped from her cup. "It will also be quite good fun to spend her father's money." She laughed and raised her cup in a toast.

"Jolly good. I am so pleased. The church is already booked. Tommy took care of that. Maisie already has her dress, and it is absolutely beautiful." She took a sip. "What do you think that we should do about the reception?"

"Would we be able to raise a marquee on the village green, in case of rain?" Mrs Newton leaned her elbows on the table.

"I would have to ask the parish council, but perhaps." Mrs B sat back a little in her chair. She was aware that she had been nervous, and could finally take a breath, now that Mrs Newton was involved.

20.

Mrs B finds a marquee

"Good morning, Mrs Lennet. I am so sorry to bother you. I wonder if you might have a few minutes you could spare?" Mrs B stood in the yellow morning room, where the butler had led her.

"Mrs B. I am so pleased to see you. I was just about to have my morning coffee. Would you join me, or would you rather have tea?" Mrs Lennet held out her hand to Mrs B, and showed her to a comfortable chair.

"Thank you. I would like to try some coffee." Mrs B waited while Mrs Lennet arranged the refreshment. "I wondered if you might be able to help me."

"I will if I can. What do you need?" The door opened and a young girl Mrs B recognised from the village carried in a tray very carefully. "Thank you, Jane."

"Good morning, Jane. How is your mother?" Mrs B turned in her seat.

"Very well, thank you, Mrs B." Jane left the tray

and hurried from the room.

Mrs Lennet passed her a cup of coffee. Mrs B sipped carefully. It was bitter on her tongue, but she liked it. "Thank you, Mrs Lennet. It seems that I like coffee." Mrs B smiled across at her hostess. "The reason I am bothering you today is that I remembered that you have a marquee here for the village fayre. I wondered if it would be possible to borrow it for a wedding?"

"Oh my, when is your big day to be?" Mrs Lennet clasped her hands together.

"Oh no, it's not for my wedding, that is yet to be arranged. This is for Maisie and Tommy. It is to be a large wedding, and Maisie's mother wondered if we might be able to put up a marquee on the village green in case of rain." Mrs B sipped her coffee, savouring the taste.

"I should think that would be fine. Of course, I will have to check with my husband, but I think he will be absolutely happy with it." Mrs Lennet looked over her shoulder to check that the door was closed. "I took your advice and discussed the plan for the year ahead with my husband. We are learning to work together. Also, Mr Trot has been interesting. The top field it almost entirely covered in pig dung and straw. It smells ghastly, but we will be able to plough it in soon and the smell and the soil might improve." She reached across to take Mrs B's hand. "I am so grateful for all your advice. May I give you a little of mine?"

"Your advice? Yes, of course." Mrs B set her cup down carefully.

"You love Will, and he loves you. Why wait? Grab your chance at happiness while you can." Mrs Lennet squeezed Mrs B's hand.

"Thank you, Mrs Lennet. I believe Will would agree with you. It is me who holds back from marriage. May I speak frankly?" Mrs B wrapped her hands around each other in her lap.

"Yes, indeed, I hope so. You have been such a wonderful friend. I hope you do not need to ask." Mrs Lennet sat forward.

"When I married my first husband, we were very young. I thought I loved him, but this is very different. I am entirely overwhelmed by how I feel. Will is wonderfully patient, but I am afraid of the strength of feelings that I am experiencing." Mrs B reached for her coffee and sipped.

"Mrs B, I believe that you and I can solve this problem. In fact, I think we are entirely best placed to do so. Please do not worry. Allow me to help you, as you have helped me." Mrs Lennet smiled widely. "Finish your coffee, my dear. You and I have work to do."

21.

Mrs B takes advice

"Mrs B? You are a wonderful person, but if I may, I think you perhaps have forgotten something along the way?" Mrs Lennet settled back into the soft leather of the car seat.

Mrs B sat next to her. If she was worried that she had no idea where they were going, she gave no such impression. She checked her handbag and that her handkerchief and purse were tucked inside. She raised her eyes to meet Mrs Lennet's. "No, I think I have everything."

"Ah, here we are, Mrs B." Mrs Lennet turned to address the driver. "Thank you. We will be at least two hours." He nodded his understanding and opened the back door for Mrs Lennet and Mrs B to step onto the pavement.

The shop they entered was unlike any that Mrs B had ever visited. There was nothing in the window that suggested what would be on sale inside. It was really very perplexing.

"Ladies, good morning. Mrs Lennet, it's a pleasure to see you again. Please come through."

The sales woman was beautifully dressed and Mrs B could not see a hair out of place. She followed Mrs Lennet and the assistant through to a private room. "I have some items to show you, as discussed. Mrs B, I understand from Mrs Lennet that you are one of her friends. I am going to ask you please to trust me." The young woman reached for Mrs B's hands and held them tightly.

"Very well. I must admit that I am rather nervous now." Mrs B allowed herself to be led away. She closed her eyes, as requested, and felt a dress being slipped over her head. Her feet were eased into shoes and her hat removed, she was led out, her eyes still closed.

"Open your eyes." Mrs Lennet stood to the side. Mrs B saw her reflection in the three biggest mirrors she had ever seen. Her practical skirt and coat were gone, and she wore a beautiful dress made of satin. Her hair had been freed from its usual bun and was raised into a stylish chignon. She turned carefully, watching the way the fabric moved. The dress fell to just below her knee, and the skirt was wide, the fabric was a delicate cream. The shoes matched the soft cream colour of the dress. She looked entirely different. Stylish and confident.

"Oh my. Mrs Lennet. What did you do?" Mrs B turned to her friend.

"I told you that you had forgotten something. It

was that you're a beautiful woman. You deserve to be loved and to love right back. Will is a lucky man to have you." Mrs Lennet wiped a tear. "I suggest that you try a few more on, just to be sure, but I really think this is the dress for your wedding."

"Oh my. I am not certain that I could. I mean, it seems frighteningly expensive." Mrs B turned to the saleswoman and back to Mrs Lennet.

"Indeed, it is, but as it is my treat, there is no cause for alarm." Mrs Lennet sat back down in the small chair. She turned her attention to the assistant. "Do you have some other dresses for my friend to try?"

22.

Mrs B seeks approval

The small church in Little Mellington waited quietly for her. The sunlight filtered through the stained glass in the windows and picked up the dust motes that drifted there.

She slid into the pew, which she had always thought of as her own; she had sat there first with her parents and her sister, and later with her husband. Sometimes with her sister and her husband and their son. Recently, with Arnold and Barbara and their daughter Jennifer, and then with Maisie. She felt her face move into a smile. So much love. That was all it was. She knew that she had been lucky. That she had been surrounded by people who loved and cared for her all of her life.

This church had been important to her. She had been christened with water from the font at the back of the church. She had knelt at the altar to receive the blessing of the Bishop when she took her confirmation. This was the church where she had married, and where she had mourned her husband. A memorial service, to say goodbye even though no body had come home. This was the home of her soul, just as her cottage was the home of her body. When she was troubled, or worried, or sad, this was the place she came to, and it had never once let her down.

The peace of the place filtered into her soul and her heart. She folded her hands in her lap and sat back against the sun warmed wood of the pew.

Maisie and Tommy's blessing was planned, and everything was ready for the big day. Mrs B ran through the lists in her mind. She thought her way through the plans.

Mrs Newton had been more helpful than she had imagined possible. Mrs B had been amazed at her happy smile and the lightness of her step. Perhaps she was truly excited for Maisie and Tommy, and looking forward to the wedding. The planning had gone more smoothly that she had expected.

The date had been set and it would only be a week until the big day. Mrs B's hands were still clasped around each other. Once Maisie and Tommy's day was over, what was stopping her from arranging her own celebration?

One day, she would walk down the aisle in the dress that Mrs Linnet had taken home in a box, and find Will waiting for her at the altar. Perhaps it would be sooner rather than later. She had, she believed, said goodbye to the fears and ghosts of her first marriage. Her eyes closed, the light bright against her eyelids.

In her mind, she searched for a picture of her husband. Not one that she had in a frame at home, where he had been posing, concentrating all his efforts on looking serious. One that she had in her mind, that nobody else had seen. The smell of him, fresh soap and ironed cotton. The touch of his hand on hers, and his gentle kiss. His love. She rested her hand on the back of the pew in front of her and took a breath.

"Wish me luck, Herbert." She patted the wood beneath her hand, stood and bowed her head to the altar. The sun outside was bright after being inside the church. Her steps, taken in far more sensible shoes than the ones Mrs Lennet had taken home on Mrs B's behalf, wrapped in tissue paper and safe within their box, took her to the gate and out onto the lane.

"Mrs B?" Mr Trot stood in the lane.

"Mr Trot? It has been a while." She took another few steps to draw level with him. "How are you?"

"I need a few minutes of your time, if you can spare them?" Mr Trot squeezed the hat he held between his fists.

23.

Mrs B receives a gift, and a question

"Mr Trot? How can I help?" Mrs B slipped the handle of her handbag into the crook of her elbow.

"I have found out something today. It was a surprise." He twisted his hat between his hands. "I know what you think of me, what the whole village thinks. It's true that I have not always been honest. Some of my trading has been underhanded. I admit that. But what I discovered today is something new to me."

"Whatever could it be, Mr Trot?" Mrs B tipped her head to one side. She watched him transfer his weight from one foot to another. "I always find that when there is something I am finding it difficult to say, it is best to have a cup of tea in my hand. Do you find that?" She pointed up the lane. "My cottage is just up the hill. Perhaps we might have a cup of tea and discuss whatever it is that is on your mind?"

Back in her kitchen, Mrs B soon had two steaming cups on the table. "Here we are. How about a biscuit to go with it?" She pushed the plate across the table.

Mr Trot took a sip and nodded. "Good tea."

"Yes, indeed," Mrs B watched him choose a biscuit and snap it between his fingers.

"Mr Lennet, up at the big house, he asked me to supply manure to make those top fields of his productive. He paid me to spread it too. I earned the money. It was honest work. Strange thing was that he told me this morning, when I went to pick up this week's money, that you recommended me." He took a sip. "To the best of my knowledge, nobody has ever done that before."

"I may have mentioned that you might be able to help them, but I am certain that they would not have continued to use your services unless you had provided them with what was required. I believe you have this work almost entirely based on your own merit." Mrs B took a biscuit from the plate.

"That was not the thing I found." Mr Trot chewed the biscuit in his mouth and swallowed. "I found that I have a friend. I know an awful lot of people, but I wouldn't call them friends." He stopped to sip his tea. "If ever you need any help. I will be your friend too." He pulled a small posy from his pocket. Some of the stems were bent, and the blooms were a little bruised, but he presented it to her with pride.

Mrs B accepted the gift with the gravity it deserved. She had been lucky, blessed with many people she would have described as friends. It seemed that Mr Trot had not been so fortunate. "Thank you, Mr Trot. You are most kind. I am glad to have made a friend, too."

He nodded and pushed his hat back onto his head. "Thank you for the tea." He smiled, showing an alarming number of missing teeth, and he was gone.

"Well, there is a surprise." Mrs B told Marmalade as he wound his soft body around her leg. "I shall have to put these in some water, I think."

24.

Mrs B and the Newlyweds

"Mrs B? Are you at home?" Maisie's voice floated up the stairs.

"Maisie?" Mrs B hurried down the stairs. "Tommy? Oh my, I am so pleased to see you both. I have missed you." She wrapped her arms around them. Slowly, she pulled back. "Married life seems to suit you both."

"Tommy has made me so very happy, Mrs B. But you know what he is really not very good at?" Maisie smiled across the hallway as Mrs B shook her head. "He makes really rubbish tea."

Mrs B raised her eyebrows at Tommy. "Come along, both of you. I will teach you how to make tea." Mrs B led them into the kitchen. "Now, you must tell me where you have been. Everything is ready for the wedding. I hope that you approve of the arrangements."

"You have done all that for us? That is so kind. Thank you." Tommy reached for her hands. "I have something I want to ask you. Maisie and I have talked about it, and if you agree, I would like you to be my best man, or best woman, if that is possible?"

"I would have thought you would ask one of your friends." Mrs B struggled with her tears, and gave up.

"I have. You're my best friend, Mrs B." He watched her wipe her tears.

The kettle came to a boil with a whistle. "I had better make that tea and find some biscuits if we are to celebrate my being a best man." She patted his hand gently. "You are very kind to ask me, Tommy. My friend. I'm very honoured."

She put the steaming cups in front of them and watched Maisie sip. "Oh, now that is a cup of tea." She laughed at Tommy's expression. "Come on, tell us about the plans you have made for the blessing. I'm so excited."

"You have cut it close. There are only two days to go. I hope that you agree with my choices. We would be hard pressed to change much now." Mrs B smiled across the table. "I will fetch the lists and show you what has been done."

25.

Mrs B and the Best Day

"Tommy? Are you awake?" She tapped on the door to her spare bedroom.

"Yes, I am. Come on in." He was sitting up in bed when she opened the door.

"I brought you breakfast. Best Man's duties." She laughed. "Maisie is a wonderful girl. You both look so happy. I'm proud of you, Tommy McKinley."

He sat back against the cushions and took the tray that she passed to him. "This reminds me of the day I was injured and you stitched my wounds up. You and I have been through some interesting times, haven't we?" He shovelled a fork loaded with scrambled egg into his mouth.

"We have indeed, Tommy and the biggest adventure is about to begin." She shook her head. "Or at least it will if you can get up out of your bed. There is hot water ready for you, and you have an hour to get clean, shaved and dressed."

He looked up from the nearly empty plate. "Only an hour?"

"Yes, I left you to sleep. Come along, now. I want you to arrive at the church clean and tidy." Mrs B left him to finish his breakfast.

Downstairs, she listened to the sounds of him moving around upstairs. Two ideas chased around her head. The first was that she would grow used to the sound of a man moving about upstairs when Will moved in to her house. The second was that she would need to find out why Mrs Newton was being so secretive about the gentleman friend she was bringing to the wedding.

26.

Mrs B meets Mrs Newton's friend

The village was so very busy. Tommy walked through the crowd, stopping to greet friends and relations on the way. Mrs B followed in his wake and watched with pride the confident young man he had become.

Mrs B greeted neighbours and good friends as she made her way through the crowd. The smile that stretched her face she saw echoed on theirs. Later, she would not remember what those people said to her, or who hugged her. She would remember the feeling, though. The wave of love and joy that met her and Tommy on their journey into the churchyard was a little overwhelming.

A flash of turquoise close to the church caught her eye. Mrs Newton's dress was not a shade Mrs B would have chosen, but everyone's taste was different.

Somebody pushed past Mrs B, and turned to apologise. "Oh, thank goodness. Mrs B, I was looking for you. I need your help." Mrs

Anderson's hand was wrapped tightly around Mrs B's.

"Whatever is it, Mrs Anderson?" Mrs B steered the distracted woman away from the crowd.

"He's back. My brother-in-law." Mrs Anderson's fingers worried at her sleeve.

"Is he at your house?" Mrs B tipped her head to one side.

"No. He's back with Mrs Newton. At the wedding. She's wrapped around him like a bandage." Mrs Anderson shook her head.

"Oh my. Right, leave this to me." Mrs B made her way through the throng. "Mrs Newton? Mrs Newton? How well you look in that dress. May I have a moment?"

When Mrs Newton turned towards her, Mrs B noticed that she did not remove her hand, which rested in a proprietorial manner on a man's arm. "This must be your friend, Mr Anderson. How very good to meet you." Mrs B held out her hand.

"Yes. This is Percy Anderson." Mrs Newton's voice was softer than usual.

"May I borrow you for a moment? There is something that we must discuss, Mrs Newton." Mrs B smiled up at Mr Anderson.

With regret, Mrs Newton allowed herself to be moved away. "Maisie will be here shortly with her father. If he arrives and finds Mr Anderson here, there will be a scene. You are her mother. I am standing in place for a best man. It is our job to make this the best day possible for Maisie and Tommy. Please, I am begging you to ask him to leave before all hell breaks loose." Mrs B wrapped her hands around Mrs Newton's. "I know that having a new man in your life has lifted your spirits, and there is a part of you that is looking forward to showing Mr Newton that someone else wants you." She watched her comments hit home. "But you are so much better than that. I have been lucky to work alongside you while we have planned this wedding, and I know that you are a better, stronger person than that."

Mrs Newton took a deep breath. "Of course, you're right. I was looking forward to rubbing Tony's nose in it." She shook her head. "Stupid of me. Today is Maisie's day. Leave it to me." She turned away and Mrs B watched her step over the uneven grass towards Mr Anderson. He bent his head to listen, and his eyes met Mrs B's unflinching gaze over her shoulder.

The way he held his head, the tightness around his jaw, the angry steps that he took towards the gate, and the regret on Mrs Newton's face when she turned back towards the church. All of these facts were not lost on Mrs B. Neither was the angry look that he shot over his shoulder at her. Battle lines, it seemed, had been drawn.

"Look, here is Mr Newton's car. I will leave you

to have a word with Maisie." Mrs B wrapped her arms around Mrs Newton. "I will see you inside."

Mrs B paused in the doorway long enough to see Mr Newton help Maisie out of the car. She looked more beautiful than she ever had.

Tommy was waiting at the front of the church, standing alone. "Where have you been?" He hissed a whisper.

"I have been avoiding some problems before they happened. Or at least postponing them until after your wedding." Mrs B leaned in close to him.

"Bad problems?" His eyebrows lifted towards his hairline.

"Bad enough." The organ music swelled and filled the church. Mrs B tapped Tommy on the arm. "Your bride has arrived. There will be time enough to worry about these things after the wedding." She smiled up into the face that had become so dear to her. "You are a lucky man, Tommy McKinley."

27.

Mrs B and the Blessing

Mr Newton's smile was wide enough to for Mrs B to worry about permanent damage to his usual scowl. He stood at the church door with Maisie. Her dress slipped and slithered its silky way around her curves and was so white it almost sparkled in the church.

Mrs B looked behind her. Mr McKinley was the only person in the church not looking at Maisie. He was looking at his son. Distracted, he realised that Mrs B had seen him. He smiled and turned to watch his daughter-in-law.

Mrs B felt Tommy's sharp intake of breath. It was exactly the reaction she had hoped for. Maisie and her father set off up the short aisle and the church filled with gasps and sighs. She was surely the most beautiful bride ever.

Reverend Chambers stood to greet them as they arrived at the front of the church. "Hello Tommy." She whispered.

"Hello. It's nice to see you." He smiled down at her.

"Wouldn't have missed it for the world." She reached for his hand and squeezed.

Mr Newton stepped back and sat down. Mrs B watched the whole service, but could not remember the words, which was unusual for her. She was so mesmerised by the two young people beside her.

When Tommy and Maisie walked out of the church, Mrs B held back. She was pleased to see that both Mr Newton and Mr McKinley were chatting and smiling. Mrs Newton stood to one side, and for the first time since they had met, she seemed entirely at a loss as to her next step.

"Mrs Newton?" Mrs B offered an arm to her. "Would you walk out with me? I really have no wish to go alone." Mrs B waited for Mrs Newton to think about it.

"I should like that very much. Thank you, Mrs B." Without a backward glance, Mrs Newton linked her arm through Mrs B's and together they left the church.

Mrs B caught Will's eye as she walked. His smile warmed her heart, and the words he had whispered the night before brought a tear to her eye. "Us next." He had said. Yes, indeed. They would be next.

28.

Mrs B meets Mr Anderson

The marquee was gaily lit with the lights that usually adorned the village hall at Christmas, and the band that had been playing since the happy couple led their guests out of the church and into the marquee was still keeping the guests dancing. The sun had set long before, but nobody seemed in the mood to go home. Mrs B watched Tommy lead Mrs Newton between the tables to dance with her, laughing with her as they danced.

"I need some air, Will. It's stuffy in here." She smiled at his offer to go with her, but shook her head.

Mrs B stood by the entrance, watching the celebrations, pleased with the way that it had gone. Relieved that the men who worked for Mr McKinley and Mr Newton had behaved with incredible restraint. There had not been a single angry word from either side. It was miraculous.

"My brother's wife told me that you were kind to them, but having her send me away was unkind.

What am I to think?" He stood just outside the circle of light.

"Mr Anderson? You are surely aware that your presence here is bound to cause great upset. My only goal was to give Tommy and Maisie a peaceful day to look back on." She turned towards the darkness.

"You do not approve of my returning to Mrs Newton." He breathed out a stream of cigarette smoke.

"I think it will bring danger and fear for you and many others." She moved her handbag into the crook of her elbow. "I hope that your love for each other makes that worthwhile."

"Love?" His laugh carried a gust of cigarette smoke towards her.

"It must be to risk such danger." Mrs B watched his face in the shadows.

"I have earned a living in many ways since I left here. Sometimes as a musician. Other times I have worked in less honourable professions." He laughed. "She's good enough for me. Neither of us are children. You can take that shocked expression off your face. She knows as well as I do that this is no fairy story."

"I think that you might be incorrect. Mrs Newton knows better than anyone the fury that will be set loose by your presence. She would not risk it lightly." She waited for his answer, and turned back to him, when he stayed silent. "Unless I am very much mistaken, she cares very much for you."

"I am in need of certain things. All of which she has. You and she are very different." He dropped his cigarette and ground it under his heel. "She has a warm house and provides regular meals and there are some extra bonuses." He shrugged and pulled another cigarette out of the packet. She watched his face, lit by the flare of the match.

"I am trying to work out whether you are as unfeeling as you pretend, or if you think you should be." She turned back to the party at the sound of Will's voice calling her. "Either way, I believe your regard for your own self-preservation will mean that you leave Mrs Newton to enjoy her daughter's wedding. Good evening to you, Mr Anderson."

Will was waiting for her by the table. His hand was warm as he led her into a space and took her in his arms to dance to the music. "Nice to be dancing with the most beautiful girl in the room." He smiled down into her eyes.

"Maisie's over there, you fool." She laughed.

"I know where Maisie is, and I am dancing with the prettiest girl here." He leaned down and kissed her cheek while she laughed, shaking her head.

29.

Mrs B's new investigation

Marmalade had insisted that Mrs B get up and make breakfast. Although this was not unusual, a late night of dancing at a wedding was, and her feet were paying the price.

Arnold pushed open the back door and found her at the table with a piece of toast and a cup of tea. "Hello? How did the wedding go? They were taking down the marquee when I drove past."

"Hello Arnold. It was rather wonderful. I do love a wedding. There's tea in the pot if you have time." She sipped from her own cup.

"Sorry, no I don't. I need your help, Auntie. There has been a murder and none of the officers have any ideas. Can you help?" He leaned against the kitchen table.

"Of course. I will fetch my coat." She looked down at her feet in the soft slippers and took a breath. "And my shoes."

Arnold drove them to the less expensive end of Potterton. The houses there were closer together, and many had been divided into flats. The building they parked outside had a scrubby front garden, which nobody seemed to take care of, and a jumble of doorbells by the front door.

"We are heading to the middle flat." Arnold fumbled with the keys. He let them in and they climbed the stairs together. One flight up, he unlocked another door and showed her inside. "I'll tell you all we know. The man was found face down on the floor here. He died from blood loss. The flat had been pulled apart. Presumably they were searching for something. The neighbours heard some shouting and banging late in the evening, but nothing after that. The victim was employed at a nightclub as door staff. We found cash and a gold chain which would suggest that robbery was not the motive. The door was locked and the key was on the floor next to the body." Arnold stopped to look at Mrs B. "He might have been having some money problems. The landlord found him when he came round to collect the overdue rent. He had a spare set of keys."

"But you found cash?" Mrs B stepped carefully around a chair.

"Yes. Not a great deal, but enough to cover the rent, I would have thought." Arnold shrugged.

"Which nightclub?" Mrs B looked down at the stain on the carpet.

"The Carousel, in Linton Street." Arnold shook

his head. "Not the most upmarket venue, but they keep the customers from making trouble. There's a fight now and then, but usually they deal with it before we have to be involved."

"Perhaps that is the place to start looking." Mrs B walked slowly through the rest of the flat, checking for permission to open the cupboards and drawers. In the small kitchen, she bent down to look into the small cupboards, and tilted her head to the side. "This might be something?"

"What do you have?" Arnold came through and joined her to look at the cupboard.

"No. Here." She pointed to the bottom of the drawer above. An envelope was taped to the base of it.

"Let's take a look." Arnold reached for the envelope and removed the tape. He ran his finger under the flap. "It's sheet music. Why would anyone hide that?"

"I suspect that is what we need to find out, Arnold." Mrs B looked at the sheets in his hand. She was no musician, and the notes on the sheet mean nothing to her. She would need to find someone who could decipher them.

30.

Mrs B visits a nightclub

The building was in need of a coat of paint. Mrs B stood outside to evaluate the place. "What was his name, Arnold?"

"The victim?" She nodded. "Mathew Brunswick."

"My experience of nightclubs is limited. Would he have stood at the door and decided who would be allowed in?" She rested her hand on the handle of the front door. It was brass, but nobody had polished it.

"Yes, there would be a team of them, a couple on the door, others inside to stop any trouble before it got out of hand." Arnold knocked hard on the door, and they watched an elderly gentleman shuffle towards them. He pointed to the sign that declared the premises closed. "Police. Open up." Arnold shouted. The man leaned his mop against the wall and unlocked the door.

"I'm not allowed to let anyone in." He told them.

"A man who worked here, Mathew Brunswick. Do you know him?" Arnold stepped past the man and walked on the freshly mopped floor, which brought tutting noises from both the man and Mrs B.

"Matt? He works the door. Nice guy, always friendly with the punters." He nodded to himself.

"Was he good friends with anyone, or had he argued with anyone that you know of?" Arnold pulled out his notebook and checked the time on his watch.

"Door staff are always arguing with people. Sometimes they can't let someone in, because they're already drunk or they've been in a fight here before. No arguments with the staff. He was mates with everyone." He took a breath. "What's he done?"

"Excuse me. Mr?" Mrs B stepped forward.

"Sid Merryn." The man turned towards her, clearly not certain why she was there.

"Are there any members of staff who have left recently? Or been fired?" She watched him think about it.

"One of the barmaids left to get married a couple of weeks ago. The cloakroom girl left, too. Not sure why. Musicians are always changing, they get a few pennies more somewhere else, they're off." He ticked off the list on his fingers.

"Right, I will be back later and I'll have more questions. Thank you for your time, Mr Merryn."

Arnold caught a hard look from his aunt. "Sorry about the floor."

Back in the car, Mrs B was quiet. "I need to find someone who can read this music. It must be important to have been hidden." She nodded to herself. "We need to call in on Mr Phelps. He can read it."

Arnold drove back to Little Mellington and parked the car outside the church. He followed Mrs B across the lane towards a small cottage, where she knocked on the door.

"Mrs B?" The man who answered the door wore heavily framed glasses which had slipped down his nose.

"Mr Phelps. I wonder if I might ask you to play a piece of music for me?" She passed him the sheet music.

"My pleasure. Please come in. Hello Arnold, how are you?" They followed him through the cluttered living room and waited while he scanned through the notes on the paper. He sat down at the piano and played a piece of music that neither of them recognised but was hauntingly beautiful. "This is very good. Who wrote it?"

"I have no idea, Mr Phelps. I was hoping that you might be able to tell me something about it." Mrs B smiled across at her old friend.

"I can tell you that whoever wrote it was very talented. More than that, perhaps. I would love to see more of their work if you come across it." He handed back the papers reverently. "Oh, hang on. There's something on the back." He turned the middle sheet over. His brows furrowed. "It says 'Run P. He knows.'"

"How very strange. Thank you, Mr Phelps. I shall let you know if I find any further compositions." Mrs B smiled.

"P isn't Matthew Brunswick unless he had a nickname. Perhaps Mr Brunswick is the "he" who knew?" Arnold's brow furrowed as he opened the car door for his aunt.

"I wonder. You may be correct, or our Mr Brunswick might be the person who warned "P", I suppose?" She turned in the seat to look at Arnold. "You said that he bled to death. Was that from one cut or several?"

"Oh, more than several. Many." Arnold cleared his throat.

"Right, I need some more information, but I also need some time to think. Might I give you a list, Arnold?" He nodded, and drove her home, leaving her to put on the kettle while he took his list away.

31.

Mrs B makes a connection

"Hello Arnold. Did you find out the answers I needed?" Mrs B poured him a cup of tea.

"I have arranged for the rest of the door staff to come in an hour earlier tonight so that we can talk to them. The cloakroom girl left two weeks ago. Her name is Maureen. There was a rumour doing the rounds that she was seeing the Assistant Manager." He flipped the notebook closed.

"What about the musicians?" Mrs B sipped her tea.

"Three have left in the last month. I should be able to collect the names when we go to talk to the door staff." He helped himself to a biscuit.

"I need to go to Mrs Pendle's to catch up on my work." She left him to finish his tea. "I won't be long."

At Mrs Pendle's house, Mrs B found the kitchen in its usual mess. She quickly set about cleaning up and was just wiping down the surfaces when her friend arrived home. "Mrs B. I really didn't expect you. Not after all the work you put in to Maisie's wedding. It was a wonderful day, wasn't it?" Mrs Pendle deposited her son on the rug and watched him laughing and kicking his legs. "Thank you for popping in. I have a little news while you're here." Mrs Pendle rested her hand on her stomach. "It seems that while I may have been a slow starter, I shall be giving Grizelda a run for her money this year."

"Another baby? Oh, my word, how exciting! Congratulations, Mrs Pendle. I am so very pleased for you." Mrs B gave her a hug and smiled.

"You won't tell anyone? Not until I'm a little further along." Mrs Pendle stood back from the embrace.

"Perish the thought that I would ever betray a confidence." Mrs B stood completely still. "That's it. Thank you, Mrs Pendle. I will see you very soon. Take good care of yourself." Mrs B left Mrs Pendle and rushed back up to her cottage, where Arnold waited.

They drove to the nightclub in silence while Mrs B's fingers worried at the handle of her handbag. Could she be mistaken? Of course she could.

32.

Mrs B meets the staff

Arnold held open the door, and they were greeted by five enormous men.

"Good evening, gentlemen. I wonder if you could help me gather some thoughts in my mind." Mrs B accepted the chair that had been fetched for her. "Tell me what you thought of Mathew Brunswick, if you please?"

"Matt was a good friend. If there was trouble on the door or inside, he never just left you to it. He always made sure we were alright." The young man held out his hand and took Mrs B's in his. "I heard what they did to him. Terrible thing."

"They?" Mrs B watched his face.

"One on one, Matt would have fought back. There had to be more than one, maybe more than two." He turned to his companions, who nodded their agreement.

"Thank you. Now what do you know about Maureen?" Mrs B sat back in the chair and waited.

"She left a couple of weeks ago. I'll be honest, I

thought she was a bit stuck up." He shifted his weight from one foot to another. "Pretty girl, though."

"Was she seeing anyone who worked here? Could Mr Brunswick have been taking her out?" Mrs B tipped her head to one side.

"Not Matt. But yes, there was talk that she was seeing Jamie, the Assistant Manager. I know Matt was worried about her when she gave in her notice. He said she'd been playing games with the wrong people, something like that." His eyes slid towards his colleagues, who all seemed to agree with his memory.

"Thank you, I'm sorry I missed your name." Mrs B waited.

"Ben Grainger." He nodded.

"Thank you, Mr Grainger. You have been helpful. Does anyone else remember anything else that happened?" They all shook their heads. "What about the musicians?"

"They come and go. The band leader puts out an advert for a saxophone player or a drummer and one turns up. They change places all the time. Maureen was friendly with the musicians. More than with us or the bar staff." He studied his fingernails. "There was something about her, like she thought she was a step above." He shrugged. "Perhaps I'm speaking out of turn."

"Not at all. I am trying to find out why someone would do this terrible thing to Mr Brunswick, and your help is very much appreciated." She smiled up at the young man. "Tell me, is there anyone working at the club that you instinctively do not trust?"

"It's a club. People come and go. Some of the kitchen staff are only here five minutes. The thing is, you can't trust them to be on your side. That's why Matt was different. We believed in him." He held his hands out in front of him as though he would dampen the words. "I don't want any of us ending up like Matt."

"I understand that. Thank you." Mrs B turned to look at Arnold. "Can you get the names for me, of the musicians?" He nodded and let himself through the double doors.

"Is there anyone who works here who has a name that starts with P?" Mrs B watched the expressions on their faces.

"Jamie, his surname is Peters. There's a barmaid called Penny. Not sure about the names of the musicians. They usually go by nicknames, anyway. But they all seem to know each other."

"Thank you. You have been most helpful. What time do the musicians usually arrive?" She slipped the handle of her handbag into the crook of her elbow.

"Usually, ten minutes after they should." He

huffed a laugh. "They're supposed to be here before we open, but they're always late." He left her in the foyer to wait for Arnold.

"I have the names, Auntie. It's going to be a while before the musicians arrive. Are you alright to wait?" He held his notebook in his hand.

"Are the kitchen staff in?" He nodded. "Wonderful. Let's have a chat with them."

The kitchen was already busy. The food smells reminded Mrs B that she had not eaten since breakfast. She watched for a moment and spotted a young girl who was elbow deep in suds. "Excuse me. I'm here with the Police. I wondered if you might spare me five minutes?" The girl looked to the chef in the centre of the kitchen, who waved her away. Mrs B led her out of the bustle and noise of the kitchen, and Arnold found chairs for them to sit down. "May I ask your name?"

"I'm Mel Johnson." The girl's accent was not what Mrs B had expected, and the surprised must have shown on her face. "This job is to keep me fed until I can find a better one. My parents wanted me to marry someone ghastly. I have decided to find my own way instead." She studied her fingernails for a moment. "My father does not enjoy that sort of behaviour. Which is why I am working here, out of sight, so to speak."

"Well, whilst I commend your independence,

I wonder if this might not be a very tough environment." Mrs B tipped her head to one side.

"Perhaps. Still, I'm learning, and I'm not married to the dreaded Leonard!" She laughed. It was a genuine sound and Mrs B could not help but join in.

33.

Mrs B finds the elusive P

"Do you have a sample of Mr Brunswick's handwriting, Mr Grainger?" Mrs B had tracked him down in the staff room.

"Sure. He wrote the staff rotas." He pointed to the piece of paper pinned to the notice board.

Mrs B studied the way the letters were formed. She was no handwriting expert, but it seemed very similar to the writing on the back of the sheet music.

Mrs B was still no closer to working out who the intended recipient of Mr Brunswick's note was. She surely had her work cut out.

"Hello, Auntie, I have the names for you." Arnold passed her a piece of paper.

"Jolly good. That's wonderful." She took the paper that he passed her. "Oh my. Well, we have at least one candidate. I suggest we find out from Mr Peters where Maureen has gone."

The small office was cramped. All the available space was taken up with a desk and one chair.

The in and out trays overflowed. Behind the piles of paperwork, they found Mr Peters. "Matt Brunswick?" He took a breath. "How sure are you?"

"Mr Peters, we do not have time to waste. Please tell me where Maureen is." Mrs B leaned on his desk and met his glare.

"I can tell you where she is not. She is not in the flat I rented for us when I left my wife for her." He dropped his head into his hands. "She left me a note." He pulled it out and passed it across.

"It was fun. I just found a bigger payday. Take care. Mo." Mrs B read it aloud and turned to look at Arnold. "We need to speak to the musicians."

The small band was busy setting up. "A moment of your time, please, gentlemen?" They turned towards Arnold. "I need you to answer a few questions."

"Which of you found the note? The one that said 'Run P. He knows.'" Mrs B waited for them to look straight at her.

"I did. It was on the back of some sheet music. I knew it was about Maureen. She had been seeing one of the guys in the band, and Mr Peters. I told him, and he left. I scribbled thank you on a little piece of paper and tucked them both back into the envelope. When I came in the next day, the whole thing was gone." The young man lifted his drumsticks out of their bag.

"Thank you. Come along, Arnold. We really only have a few minutes." Mrs B rushed through the double doors and pushed open the door to the kitchen. "Mel? Hurry! Come with us." The young girl pulled her hands out of the sink. Her brows scrunched together. "Come on, Maureen has told your father where to find you, I believe."

She moved fast, grabbing her coat, and they hurried out of the back door into an alleyway. Her hand found Mrs B's and together they climbed into Arnold's car.

"I don't understand what just happened. Can you explain?" Mel sat back.

"Matt was your friend, wasn't he?" Mrs B squeezed Mel's hands.

"Yes. I met him the first day, after I ran away. I told him what had happened, and he got me the job." She smiled. "He didn't want anything from me."

"He left you a note. 'Run P. He knows.' It was given to the wrong person, and they ran. The person who ran told Maureen, and she contacted your father. I believe that he paid her for the information." Mrs B chewed her lip. "Whatever Mr Brunswick had found out, Maureen seems to have confirmed your whereabouts."

"Where can I go?" Mel looked a good deal younger and less confident.

"You can come and stay with me, Pamela. You will be safe until you decide where you want to be." Mrs B turned towards her new friend.

"Pamela?" Arnold took his eyes off the road for a moment to check what he had heard.

"Yes, she is the P we have been looking for. P for Pamela, shortened to Mel to throw people off the trail. Although the other P, the one who ran, well, we will have to deal with that later. I think you will like Little Mellington, Pamela. Perhaps we should change your name again, though?" Mrs B patted her hand.

"Do you know who my father is? He's dangerous." Pamela turned in her seat to hold Mrs B's hands. "People think he's respectable, but he's not. I can't go back."

"Oh, trust me. I'm tougher than I look." Mrs B laughed, and looked out of the window as the fields raced past and they drove closer to her home.

34.

Mrs B goes visiting

"Now then, remember you are my cousin's daughter, Kitty, if anyone asks." Mrs B left Pamela with Marmalade on her lap, both of them looking so comfortable and relaxed that it brought a smile to her lips. "I will be an hour or so. Help yourself to whatever you need."

The bus ride was a pleasant distraction from the message that she needed to deliver. She spent the time thinking about everything that she had learned about Pamela's family and what would need to be done to keep her safe.

Mrs Newton's house looked no different from the way it had on her last visit. She knew that she was, however, bringing bad news.

"Good morning, Mrs B. What good timing. The kettle is already on." Mrs Newton led her guest into the living room where Mr Anderson was looking very much at home. "I'll make the tea."

"Oh, it's you again." Mr Anderson flicked the page of his newspaper.

"Yes indeed. I have had an interesting week,

and I thought you might like to hear about it. You were playing in the band at The Carousel until recently. Apparently seeing a young lady called Maureen. You were passed a note which you imagined was for you." She sat down and watched his eyebrows lift towards his hairline. "It was not for you, and neither was Maureen a very nice person. So, if you plan to stay, do so because you like Mrs Newton, not because you are in hiding." She sat forward on her chair. "I think Maureen told you that she wanted a more serious relationship or that she was expecting your baby. Something that spooked you. Perhaps you thought that Jamie Peters had discovered your affair? I really do not know. But you ran." She sat back. "Did you write the piece of music?"

Mrs Newton pushed open the door and bustled in with a tea tray. "Here we are. I hope that you two are getting along."

"Yes indeed. We were just chatting about Mr Anderson's musical talents." Mrs B accepted a cup of tea. "Lovely. Thank you. I wanted to thank you for allowing me to be involved in Tommy and Maisie's big day. It was rather marvellous."

"I was planning to say the same thing. You could have cut me out, but you asked me to be involved. I am so grateful." Mrs Newton reached for Mrs B's hands.

"Perish the thought. Maisie was far better for

having her mother there, and your advice was invaluable." Mrs B squeezed her fingers around Mrs Newton's hand.

"Please have a biscuit." Mrs Newton offered the plate.

"How kind. Yes, I think I will. Thank you." Mrs B took a small bite from the biscuit and a breath of relief. She had delivered her message and Mr Anderson could do with it as he pleased. The only worry now was what Mr Brunswick had discovered before his untimely demise.

35.

Mrs B discovers a secret

"Maureen?" The young woman looked up from the book she was reading.

"Do I know you?" Everything that she had heard about Maureen was true. She was pretty, and she thought she was better than most. Also, she was frightened.

"I know you. Mr Peters left his wife for you. Mr Anderson ran and hid because of you. You sold information to a young girl's father." She shook her head. "I think that you are in trouble, and I can help."

"What are you going to do? How can you help me?" Her eyes shone with tears.

"You might be surprised." Mrs B slid into the seat opposite Maureen. "I found you. If I can, others will not be far behind."

"Fine, I'll tell you. My husband owed a great deal of money to a very dangerous person. So much so that he had to disappear." She closed the book that she had been reading. "I don't know if he is safe or not. There was no choice but to run too, and I got a job in a run-down nightclub. I recognised the girl in the kitchen, because my husband owed the money to her father. That was it. I saw a way out. Except it wasn't." Maureen stretched her fingers on the table. "I knew he wouldn't hurt his daughter. He adores her."

"Why is it not a way out?" Mrs B reached for her hand.

"He is still chasing me for my husband's whereabouts." She breathed a sigh. "You're right. If you found me, he won't be far behind."

"I will do my best to help you. If you will let me. Do you know where your husband is? If you genuinely have no idea, then perhaps the best thing you can do is go to the police?" Mrs B felt Maureen's fingers twitch inside hers.

"He's gone and he won't be coming back." Maureen pulled her hand from Mrs B's. "I'm leaving tonight. I won't tell you where I'm going. I hope you understand." She patted Mrs B's hand. "Kind of you to want to help, though."

"Very well. Of course, it's your choice. I will wish you good luck." Mrs B looked across the table at the young woman. "I will remember you in my prayers. Stay safe, Maureen."

Mrs B walked away from the table and out into the street. There was a bus stop just a little further down the street and she waited there. When Maureen came out onto the street, she walked quickly to the train station with Mrs B ten paces behind.

An hour later, Mrs B watched as Maureen boarded a train out of town and whispered a fervent prayer that she would stay away and that nobody else would find her.

36.

Mrs B arranges an interview

"Mr McKinley? I wonder if you might spare me a few moments?" Mrs B stood on the doorstep with a basket over her arm. "I brought you some of the biscuits that you like so much."

If he was surprised to see her, he managed to hide it well. "Come on in. I always have time for your biscuits." He held the door wide open.

Inside, Mrs B followed him into the kitchen and watched while he made tea. She was happy to see that he warmed the pot first. She unfolded the paper around the biscuits and carefully placed the parcel on the table.

"I have a problem and I wondered if you might advise me as to the best way forward. Do you perhaps know a Mr Bisley?" Mrs B accepted the cup of tea that she was offered and watched Mr McKinley's expression harden at the mention of Mr Bisley's name.

"I do know him." He sat down and took a biscuit.

"I need to speak to him. It's a rather urgent matter." She sipped from her tea.

"He is a very difficult kettle of fish. Please, whatever it is, do not seek him out." He sat forward in the chair. "Please."

"The thing is, his daughter ran away. He wanted her to marry someone of his choice and it appears that the daughter refused." She sipped again. "She is staying with me."

Mr McKinley ran his hand over his face. "Oh, for the love of...right too late to tell you not to get involved. I see why Tommy says you are wonderful and infuriating in equal measure." He shook his head. "I am going to tell you a little about Mr Bisley. So that you know what you're going to have to deal with. He's clever. The man is a councillor, tipped to be mayor next year from what I hear. He made his money doing back room deals. That housing estate they're building? He pushed that through planning, and was paid a good deal to do it. I hear that he is a silent partner in the building company. The man is powerful. Not like me or Tony Newton. There is nothing upfront about him." He shook his head. "If he were to see you as a threat, it would be very bad news."

"I'm not threatening at all. I'm an infuriating old woman." She laughed, and he laughed with her. "I need to see him in public, preferably. Thank you for your advice."

"If you have to see him, then the golf club lunch

is the best place, then. It's held every Wednesday. My advice would be to speak to him before two. That way, he will be relatively sober." He chewed his lower lip. "I will drive you there and take you home again, though."

"Not at all. I shall ask my fiancee to accompany me. I am grateful for the information, though. And the tea." She stood up and left him with too much to think about and a pile of biscuits.

37.

Mrs B and Mr Bisley

"You cannot go in there alone." Will turned in his seat. "I promise not to say anything, but I must come inside." He watched the determined set of her jaw. "How about if I pretended not to be with you? I could just stay by the door or something." He uncurled his fingers from the steering wheel carefully. "I can't sit out here and worry about you."

"Fine. Come in, but wait by the door. Mr Bisley would know you from your time as a policeman. I want to keep him calm if I can." She shook her head. "He can't be as bad as all that."

"Yes, he can." Will followed her to the front door of the imposing building.

"Well, it's better if I go to him than if he comes to find me, surely." She shrugged and pushed open the door. The glass and brass were highly polished, and she felt her foot sink into the thick carpeting.

Will was as good as his word and waited by the door of the dining room where the luncheon had already been served, and the members were enjoying their brandy and cigars. Mrs B asked a passing waiter which of the gentlemen was Mr Bisley. He pointed out a slightly portly gentleman sitting at a table in the bay window. She thanked him and set off across the dining room through the cigar smoke.

"Mr Bisley? I'm so sorry to interrupt your cigar. I wondered if you might spare me a moment to have a chat about Pamela?" Mrs B watched his face change from contented and relaxed to thunderous, and then to genuine concern.

"Do you know where she is?" He leaned his hand on the tablecloth. He was a large man, his hands comfortably twice the size of hers.

"Yes, I do. The thing is, she is refusing to return home because of the marriage that she knows you wish for her. She has other plans. I wanted to let you know that she is perfectly safe and happy. I wondered if you might allow her a little time to think it all through?" Mrs B folded her hands around each other. She was well aware that he would not like the idea, but it had to be the first option.

"No. She is to come home today. I will not have her behaving this way. The wedding is on Saturday." His hands had rolled up into fists, which were white around the knuckles.

"She won't. I have asked if she would return

home and she just will not. If you insist, and you may do that, she will run away again. Next time, she may not be as lucky as she has been. There are plenty of unscrupulous people out there who might take advantage of a young girl on her own." Mrs B took a breath and shook her head at the state of the world and the evilness that could be found.

"I'm not having her running off and singing like Tony Newton's girl." He nodded when Mrs B's eyes opened wide in surprise. "Yes, I know who you are. Interfering in people's business. Let me be clear, I'm not the same as Newton. You won't worm your way into my family the same way you did with him."

"That's fair enough. I shall let Pamela know your decision." Mrs B turned away.

"So, she will be coming home tonight, then." She heard the hope in his words.

"I very much doubt it, Mr Bisley. As I said, she has no wish to marry your choice of man. I have no way of knowing where she will go to next, but I will explain that you want her to go home. I will also remind her that you love her. It is clear that you do." Mrs B turned away again.

"I'll come and pick her up from your house, then." He stood up, moving the table with his swift movement.

"Oh, she's not at my house, Mr Bisley. That

would be foolish indeed, would it not? Pamela may be many things, but she's nobody's fool." Mrs B smiled her sweetest smile and nodded her head to him. "Good day Mr Bisley. Thank you for sparing me your time."

Mrs B made it all the way to the front door, sailing past Will before he was ready to turn and follow her.

"Wait!" Mr Bisley crossed the space between them. "How long does she want to think about it?"

"Oh my, perhaps six months, maybe longer." Mrs B raised her eyes to look into his face. "I should tell you though, that no matter how long she thinks, I do not believe that she will come round to the idea of the marriage."

"Tell her she can have three months. Then I want her married. Do you understand? He's a good man. She would have a good life." His words were low and quiet.

"Indeed, I do understand. Thank you, Mr Bissey. I will ask Pamela to write you a letter and perhaps after that, you and her mother might like to meet up with her for a cup of tea? I always find that difficult conversations are easier with a cup of tea. Don't you?" She smiled and walked away. This time she kept walking, and Will was waiting for her at the front door, holding open the polished glass and brass.

"I love you." He said, opening the door of his car so that she could climb in.

Mrs B waited until he climbed into the driver's seat. "I love you too." She waited for him to drive out of the parking area, and smiled to herself as she watched the fields go by.

38.

Mrs B and Pamela

"What happened?" Pamela was waiting at the bottom of the stairs when Mrs B and Will got home.

"We need a cup of tea and I will tell you." Mrs B fussed with the kettle. While she made the tea, she recounted exactly what had been said.

"Oh, Mrs B. You are such a hero." Pamela accepted a cup of tea. "That gives me three months to convince him." She sipped. "Good tea. I can't marry Leonard. He's desperately dull. I did tell my father, right from the start, that I would not marry him."

"Why is he so determined about Leonard?" Mrs B pushed a plate of biscuits across the table.

"My father grew up in a very poor family. He did some very bad things which earned him a great deal of money, and he pushed his way into local politics. He's powerful, but those men in suits have no idea how ruthless he is. They think he is like them. He smiles and shakes hands and they all think he's a nice person. All my life, I knew that there were things I couldn't talk about. Secrets to keep." She shrugged. "He paid a good deal of money for my education. Then, as soon as I was out of school, he wanted me married off to Mr Boring. He's terrified that I will meet someone like him, and live the life he had." She wiped a tear.

"He loves you." Mrs B reached for her hand.

"Yes. Like a canary. To be kept in a cage. Not allowed freedom or choices." Pamela shook her head. "I don't want that life. I don't want the life my mum had, either. It's my own life that I want."

"Perhaps three months will not be long enough to convince him. But we can give it a jolly good try." Mrs B raised her teacup in a toast. "To freedom of choice."

"If you want to find a way to choose your own path, young Pamela, this lady is the one to help you." Will picked up his cup and clinked with theirs.

39.

Mrs B sees something surprising

"I need to earn some money. I can't just sit around. Do you think the pub might hire me to wash up the glasses or something?" Pamela took a bite from the toast that Mrs B had placed in front of her.

"I think that would be a mistake. We want your father to see you having some time to think, not working in a public house. I did hear that the doctor's receptionist was taking a few months off. I hear her mother has been very unwell, and needs help to get through the worst of her illness. Perhaps that would be a better option?" Mrs B joined her at the table.

"Looking after her mother?" Pamela's brows pushed together.

"Perish the thought, her mother is a little on the curmudgeonly side. I meant standing in for her at the doctor's surgery." Mrs B poured them both a cup of tea.

"Oh. I wonder if I could do that. I really don't have much in the way of experience." She chewed her lip.

"Let's pop down there after breakfast and see what happens?" Mrs B sipped from her cup. "Delicious."

"Excuse me, doctor?" Mrs B stood in the small reception area, where several patients were waiting. The young doctor was looking more ruffled than usual.

"Mrs B, I am trying to do three jobs at once. Can whatever it is wait for ten minutes?" He was looking through the pages of a book on the desk.

"I have come with a solution. This is Pamela, known to her friends as Kitty, who needs a job. I think you need someone to help you." She stepped sideways so that Pamela would have room to step forward.

"Oh. Well. We could try it out for today and see how we get on?" He raised an eyebrow. Pamela nodded in agreement. "Fine. These people have appointments. I have no idea where the diary is. I thought this was it, but it seems not. Perhaps that might be the first job? I also need each patient's notes so that I can write up what we are doing. Can I leave that with you? Mr Albright, would you like to come through?" He stood back to let the elderly gentleman through into his office. "Sorry, what was your name?" He met her stare across the hallway and waited for her response.

"Pamela." She moved behind the desk and started to set the mess straight.

"I will see you later. Good luck." Mrs B left her to it. Was there something in the look that had passed between the Doctor and Pamela? Or had Mrs B imagined it. She looked back at the young girl at the desk. It had been something, and it had left rosy cheeks on Pamela's face.

Out in the sunshine, a car was waiting for her. "Will? What a lovely surprise."

"You aren't unwell?" He walked around the car to wrap an arm around her shoulders.

"No, the doctor was in need of a receptionist and Pamela was at a loose end." She smiled up at him. "What are you doing here today?"

"I wondered if you were free for a picnic and a discussion about setting the date for our wedding?" He raised an eyebrow. "I made the picnic."

"That sounds wonderful, Will." She reached up and kissed his cheek. "Yes please."

40.

Mrs B makes arrangements

"Excuse me, Reverend Chambers? I wonder if you have a moment?" She had caught him as he was leaving the church.

"Of course, dear Mrs B. How may I help?" He checked his pockets to make certain that he had collected all his belongings before he left for home.

"Will and I would like to set the date." She wrapped her hands around each other.

"For your wedding? Oh my, how very exciting." His smile was wide and joyful. "Come along then, let me find the diary and we can choose a day together." She walked alongside him to his house. "I must admit that I was starting to think that you would not commit. That would have been a shame. It will be my honour to perform the ceremony." He pushed open the door to his house. "Oh my, you have been here today. I love to come home on days when you have been to the house. The smell of polish greets me on the doorstep." He smiled and held the door open for her. "Come along in, and I shall ask Mrs Chambers to make tea." He stopped in his tracks in the hallway. "Will you continue to work, Mrs B? After you are married?"

"I cannot see any reason why not, Reverend." She paused to think about it. "I have not considered anything else."

"Very good. Do come into the study, and I will find my diary." He rummaged through a drawer. "Yes, here we are. Now, I shall give you some dates that are clear, and perhaps you would need to chat with Will about which would be best for you. I know that everyone in the village will be very excited to celebrate with you."

She left with the possible dates written on a piece of paper, which she had stowed carefully in her handbag. For no reason that she could fathom, tears threatened on her walk up the lane.

When she reached her kitchen, Will and Pamela were sitting at the kitchen table chatting about the doctor's surgery and laughing. Mrs B watched them from the doorway and considered. Was she afraid of things changing? There was no need. Will had fitted into her life as though he had always been there. Then what on earth were the tears that she wanted to cry about?

"It sounds as though it's all going well at the surgery." She said and Pamela beamed at her. "I want to hear all about it. I shall put the kettle on."

"Good idea. I have something that I would like to talk to you about." Pamela sat up a little straighter and waited while Mrs B filled the kettle.

41.

Mrs B learns a little

"I have had such a wonderful day. Thank you for suggesting I help with the surgery. It's been fascinating." Her smile lifted the room.

"Wonderful. I am pleased." Mrs B sipped her tea and considered the young girl in front of her.

"I did want to ask something, though. About Matt?" She took a breath. "I think he was killed because he refused to tell someone about me. Do you think that's true?"

"To be honest, I am not certain yet. It seems likely that your father was looking for you, and anyone who stood in the way was in danger." Mrs B rested her hand on the tablecloth. "Perhaps someone who works for your father went further than they were intending to?"

"May I tell you some things about my parents? I might know something that will help find out why it happened." Her eyes swam with tears.

"You may well, but I would not ask you to compromise your family." Mrs B sipped her tea.

"I won't be. They did this to themselves." She wiped a finger under her eye and took a breath. "He's clever, always thinking. I've seen him sit absolutely still for hours on end until he can see a problem from every angle. He owns seven betting shops, and two hairdressing salons. My mother is a hairdresser, and she runs the salons. He is also part owner of four nightclubs and two boxing gyms. The money from the businesses, and the muscle from the gyms make him powerful. When he got involved in local politics, he found other business opportunities to push his way into. I've seen them when they come to the house, all dressed in suits and shaking hands politely. They don't know that they are dining with a snake who would swallow them whole if he had to." She took a breath. "Ask me anything. After what he has done, I owe him no loyalty."

"I think, if I may?" Mrs B received a nod of agreement. "He loves you. Yes, he goes about it in the wrong way, and of course, it would be better if he stepped back and allowed you to be yourself. I will be looking into his activities when Arnold picks me up this afternoon, and I am grateful for your advice. Sometimes a little background information about someone can prove most useful." She patted Pamela's hand. "I hope that you can find some middle ground to make peace with your parents."

Pamela's expression suggested that peace was

unlikely.

"Oh Will, I picked up these from Reverend Chambers for you." She pushed the folded paper across the table. He looked across at her and read the paper. "Dates when the church is free." His smile of understanding lit his face.

"Are you two getting married? How exciting! Can I be a bridesmaid?" Pamela's earlier distress evaporated across the table.

42.

Mrs B and a lucky find

The morning was bright, and there was not a cloud in the sky. Mrs B walked up the hill, enjoying the feeling of the sun on her face and the smell of the hedgerows. She reflected on the conversation she'd had after church with Mrs Lennet. Her offer to help with the wedding had been a surprise. Mrs Pendle had offered her assistance too. In fact, since the news of her impending marriage had gone around the village, she had received offers from so many people who wanted to be involved. It had touched her that they held her and her soon to be husband, in such high regard.

She was thinking about the conversation to come, and breathing a little harder as she reached the top of the hill. The car was driving too fast along such a narrow lane. She heard it before it reached her and stepped into the side of the road.

The brakes squealed in protest when the car came to an abrupt halt just a few yards after it passed her.

"Oh, here you are. I'm sorry Auntie. I know that we said this afternoon, but I am under pressure to work this out." Arnold tipped his head to the side.

"Fine. You will need to take me to Mrs Lennet's first. She is expecting me. It would be rude not to at least let her know." Mrs B walked climbed into the car.

"Right, so where do we need to go?" Arnold drove away from Mrs Lennet's home.

"I would like to visit the boxing gyms that Mr Bisley owns. Do you know where they are?" Mrs B turned in the seat to watch Arnold drive. He nodded. "I wanted to ask you something."

"Oh, yes?" He kept his eyes on the road.

"You know that Will and I have set the date for the wedding?" He nodded. "I wondered if you would like to give me away?" She watched his expression.

"Oh Auntie, I would be honoured. Thank you." He risked looking away from the road to smile at her. "Barbara is really excited about the wedding, too."

They stopped outside a rundown looking building. "Is this the place?" Mrs B pulled her handbag on to her knee. "It seems Mr Bisley is a little behind on the maintenance." She shook her head.

They walked through a long, dimly lit corridor towards the back of the building. Arnold was quick to show his police identification, and the coach signalled that it would be quieter to talk in the office. The sound of gloves pounding against punchbags and feet bouncing on the dusty floor was deafening.

Arnold leaned on the door frame. "We need to have a look around. I promise we won't be too long." The coach stood back up. "No, it's fine. We'll find our own way."

Arnold and Mrs B took a tour around the gym. If the men who were training thought it unusual for a young man and his aunt to be walking through and poking into the lockers and the changing rooms, they said nothing. It seemed it was the sort of place where saying nothing was a good idea.

They thanked the coach and walked back out into the sunshine. "Nothing in there seemed to be out of place. It was grubby, but they all seemed intent on their training. I am not certain what I expected, but I hoped I would see something, anything, that seemed wrong."

"Would you still like to see the other one?" Arnold turned to her with an eyebrow raised.

"Yes, I think so. Let's go and have a look." She settled back into the seat.

The next gym was very similar, except that there

was a parking area behind the building. They walked through the gym, but again, nothing excited their interest. On the way back to the car, they passed the rubbish bins. It seemed that they were due to be collected. The lids were balanced on the overflowing rubbish. Mrs B tutted. There really was no need to leave things so untidy.

The pair of boxing gloves were sticking out of the side, not covered by the lid. They looked reasonably new, and that in itself seemed strange.

"Arnold. These gloves seem too new to be thrown away." He joined her at the bin.

"You're right, and they're expensive to buy." He pulled the gloves out. "Oh well, that's why." Whoever had been wearing the gloves had punched something sharp, as there were cuts across the ends of the gloves. "I will put them in the car. I'm not certain how anyone could cause this sort of damage." He shrugged and pulled the gloves out of the bin. Mrs B lifted the lid so that he could pull them out. "Oh, there's another pair here. They're cut too." He pulled them out and placed them into the car.

Mrs B picked up the gloves to take a closer look. She pulled apart the leather of the gloves and looked at the cuts. "Oh my. Arnold. Look at this." She passed the glove to him.

"There's glass in the cut." He shrugged and

passed the glove back.

"What if all these cuts had a shard of glass in them, and you wore the gloves and punched someone? Would that produce similar injuries to those suffered by Mr Brunswick?" Mrs B held up the gloves to him again.

"Oh auntie. That is absolutely right." He placed the gloves carefully into the car. "We just need to find out who was wearing them."

"One step at a time, Arnold. We will have the answers soon enough." Mrs B followed him back into the gym. They had some more questions to ask.

43.

Mrs B is glad of a friend

"How will we know which ones to talk to? There must be twenty or thirty boxers in there." Arnold held the door to the gym open for his aunt.

"Arnold." She turned towards him. "If they threw away the gloves, they must have bought new ones. Let's look for the new gloves and start from there." She smiled, and they made their way inside.

Arnold walked around the gym again, picking out boxers with new looking gloves. Mrs B watched him and the boxers. When the young man near the door decided to make a run for it, she saw the decision cross his face before he moved his feet. As he reached the door, she knocked a fire bucket full of sand into his path. He tripped, skidding across the floor, and letting loose a stream of angry expletives.

"I think this gentleman is a in a great hurry to talk to you." She raised an eyebrow at Arnold.

"Thank you." He reached down and helped the young man to his feet. "Come along." Arnold clipped on the handcuffs. "We're going to need to have a good chat."

"You take him back, Arnold, and see what he will tell you. He knows something. Even if he was not there. I will take the bus home and think some more." Mrs B patted her nephew on the arm. "Take care Arnold."

The bus stopped in the village and Mrs B stepped off. She stood back and waited for the bus to drive away. She thought about whether the bakers would still have some iced buns left or if she would be too late.

The car that pulled in behind the bus was long and sleek. "Mrs B?" The passenger in the back seat leaned forward to talk out of the window. She recognised the heavy jowls and puffy eyes of Mr Bisley.

"Mr Bisley. Good afternoon to you. I hope you are well." Mrs B smiled and nodded, as though she would walk away.

"A moment of your time, please." He tapped his fingers on the car door. "You visited my boxing gyms today." He shook his head as though he was disappointed with her. "No more interfering with my business. Do you understand me?" His voice stayed a whisper, but the threat was clear.

"I can make no promises, Mr Bisley." She stepped away from the car.

"Mrs B? May I walk with you? I am going right past your cottage." Mr Trot must have been standing close enough to hear the conversation.

"Well, it is lovely to see a friendly face. Yes, that would be very kind." She stepped away and fell into step with him as they walked away, leaving a scowling Mr Bisley watching their every step.

"Keep walking, Mrs B. I may not know much, but I can spot a nasty piece of work when I see one." Mr Trot smiled across at her. "I hear you are due to be married soon. I wanted to see you anyway, to wish you every happiness. It was just my good luck to bump into you today."

"I think it was me who was lucky, Mr Trot. Indeed, I am very lucky to have a good friend in you." She smiled at him. "I hope that you will do us the honour of attending the wedding."

44.

Mrs B is followed

"He did what?" Will was angrier than she had ever seen him. "Arnold needs to arrest that man immediately. Are you alright?" He reached to wrap his arms around her.

"It's good news, don't you see? We have him worried, and that means we must be close. Arnold has the young man in custody, so I am sure we will have news soon." She rested her cheek against his chest. "I must admit that I was glad to see Mr Trot, though."

"I am so pleased that he was there. I will be sure to thank him the next time I see him." He dropped a kiss on the top of her head. I made a salad for dinner. I hope that's alright."

"It's better than alright." She fetched knives and forks. "I wonder who wrote that music though, Will. It has been running around my head. I have an idea, but I am not certain if I should pursue it. There may be people I care about who would be hurt."

"I suspect that you will think better once we have

had something to eat. Perhaps we could sit down later and go through the possibilities?" He put a plate in front of her and they ate.

"Do you know where one would buy a pair of boxing gloves around here?" She turned sideways to look at him.

"Yes. Only one place that I know of. Billingtons in Potterton High Street." He tipped his head to one side. "Do you have an idea?"

"Perhaps. Would you take me there tomorrow?" She speared a piece of tomato on her fork.

Billingtons was not a shop she had ever visited. They wandered through the shelves, which seemed to hold sporting goods for any occasion. At the back was the boxing section.

The young man who worked there was most helpful. They seemed to have sold a good deal of cricket equipment in the last month, and several tennis balls, but only two pairs of boxing gloves. They had been purchased by Mr Emerson. He ran the gym on Park Street. She thanked the young man, and they left.

"The gym on Park Street was where we found the gloves yesterday. If Mr Emerson purchased the new gloves, then it makes sense that he was involved. Certainly, Arnold needs to arrest him." She turned to Will, but he was looking the other way. "Will?"

"May I take you for a cup of tea? There's a tea shop over there." He pointed at the small shop.

"What a lovely idea." She wondered if he was a little distracted, but they ordered tea and sat together in the window.

"We were followed." He told her from behind his teacup. "Two young lads. You might recognise them from the gym if they were there yesterday."

She followed his line of vision. There was indeed a young man leaning against a corner near to Will's car. "He could have been. I'm not certain." She leaned forward. "Where's the other one?" Will kept his hand low but signalled to the left. She looked. "Oh yes. I would remember that hair." His bright red hair stuck out at all angles. "He was definitely there."

"Wonderful. It seems that Pamela was right and Mr Bisley has a network of young thugs coming up through the boxing gyms. I suppose that makes sense. It seems a big leap from watching a car to murder, though." He picked up his cup.

"Perhaps it went too far, and they panicked? They're very young, and not hardened criminals. It may be that they thought they could make Mr Brunswick tell them where Pamela was, but he refused. I still think the music is involved." She looked up to find him smiling. "What did I say?"

"I love how you worry at the edges of a problem. You will work it out." He raised his cup in a toast, and they clinked.

45.

Mrs B meets Jimmy Malone

She left the tea shop and walked quickly away from where the car was parked, tucking something carefully into her handbag. Of course, she heard the footsteps behind her, and smiled to herself, speeding up and rounding the next corner into an alleyway.

She turned back to find the young man with a mop of wild red hair grinning nastily at her. "Well, hello. I saw you yesterday, I believe, at the boxing gym? Did you need to tell me something that you forgot to mention yesterday?"

"Yes. Stay away from the gym and stop asking stupid questions. Or you'll end up in a bad way." His smile slipped when Will pushed his arm up his back and moved him up against the wall.

"I am not impressed by your behaviour. To threaten a lady is very bad manners, young man. Now, let's drop you off at the police station and see what they can make of you." Will turned him easily and marched him towards the entrance of the alley.

"Mr Bisley is already angry with you. This is only going to make him angrier." The young man struggled against Will's grip.

"You have dropped your wallet. Allow me to pick it up for you." Mrs B bent down to pick it up. "Mr James Malone. Would you be Jimmy to your friends?" She smiled and offered the wallet to him. He nodded. "I've heard of you, Jimmy Malone. Mr Bisley talked to me about you when I met him for lunch at the golf club. He said something along the lines of his not taking any of the blame for Mr Brunswick's death. He had the likes of Jimmy Malone to take the blame for things like that." She waited, watching panic and doubt compete for space on the young man's face. "No doubt you will have a long time to consider how good a friend you have been to Mr Bisley, and how he has used you."

"He wouldn't do that." The denial lacked certainty.

"Was that your friend that we picked up yesterday? He spent a night in the cells, and Mr Bisley sent no help, no lawyer. He has told his story to the police by now, I think, and yours." Mrs B stepped back to allow Will to push Jimmy Malone towards the car.

"It wasn't our fault. We were there, but we didn't kill that man." The bravado gone. His body slumped. "We just held him, to try to get him to tell us where Alan Stevens is hiding. He was being a fool. He knew how much money was owed. Nobody's going to just forget that sort of money and walk away."

"Who was hitting him then, if not you?" Mrs B watched fear and anger fly across the young face in front of her.

"Mr Emerson, and Billy Boy. They run the gym, they're in charge. I'll go to jail for holding him, won't I?" His shoulders seemed too narrow to hold the worries that rested there.

"Perhaps Jimmy. But Mr Emerson and Billy Boy will go for longer." She looked into his troubled eyes. "Tell the truth Jimmy. Stand up straight and tell the truth." He nodded. "For heaven's sake, don't let them make you take the blame for their actions."

Arnold was happy to take delivery of Jimmy Malone, and the information that he had given. He promised his aunt that Mr Emerson and Billy Boy would be in custody very soon.

"Poor boy. He really had no choice. Perhaps the judge would give less of a sentence if we were to speak for him?" Mrs B turned in her seat to look at Will as he drove.

"Perhaps, but I imagine that the best thing that we can do is get Bisley out of circulation, to stop him from coming after Jimmy or anyone else." He kept his eyes on the road. "Or you."

"I think perhaps you're right." She smiled across at him and waited for a smile in response. "We will need to connect him to Mr Emerson and Billy Boy, and prove that he instructed them to go to Matthew's place."

"Leave Emerson and the other one to Arnold. He will collect them, I'm sure." Will turned the corner, and she realised they were nearly home.

"I am looking forward to a cup of tea." Will opened the door and held her hand on the path to her back door.

Inside, she put on the kettle, and watched Will move to pick up Marmalade. "Hello little fellow. Have you been busy today?" He stroked his fingers through the thick orange and white fur.

The teapot was on the table and the cups and jug were ready, when the back door flew open. "Mrs B!" Pamela ran, breathless into the kitchen. "You have to help. Please!"

46.

Mrs B has a rushed journey

"Whatever has happened, Pamela?" Mrs B jumped to her feet and held Pamela's hands.

"My mum came to find me. She said he's gone over the top this time. He's done something terrible. I think this is my fault. It's because he's so angry with me." Pamela sank onto a chair at the table.

"Now first things first. His behaviour is his own fault, not yours. Whatever has he done?" Mrs B fetched a cup and poured a cup for Pamela.

"She said that she overhead a conversation and my father told someone to take someone to the shop. That he would make sure that they would pay." Her voice shook. "He left the house an hour ago. We have to stop him."

"We will. Come along now. Give me the address of the shop. I will go, and Will you will need to fetch Arnold." Mrs B pulled her coat on.

"You can't go alone." Will shook his head.

"I have no intention of going alone. I will wait

outside, and keep watch, so that we know for sure that nobody has left, while you fetch Arnold and the police. I promise I will not do anything risky." She reached across the table and smiled. "You are so kind to worry about me."

"I should come with you." Pamela's voice was flat.

"No, I think that might be a very dangerous thing to do. It would put your mother at risk as well. Much safer to let the police do their job." Mrs B buttoned up the coat and stroked Marmalade. "Could you feed the cat for me, please?"

Pamela passed a piece of paper to Mrs B. "He calls it the shop, but it's more like a warehouse. Please promise you'll stay out of danger."

"I will be fine. I am far tougher than I look." Mrs B gave a wide, but not entirely confident, smile.

"On the way, I am driving past Arnold's house. Why don't we stop there and ask him to bring other officers, then we can go together to the building?" Will turned to take a look at her expression.

"Yes, that might save some time. Thank you, Will." She smiled across at him.

Arnold was cutting the hedge at the front of his house when they arrived. It only took a few words to be shared for him to be running for his car keys and to shout to Barbara where he was going.

"Wait for us to arrive. Whatever happens." He shouted, slamming the car door behind him.

Will and Mrs B climbed back into Will's car and drove the last part of the journey to the address that Pamela had given them.

"I'm ever so glad that we're going together." Mrs B reached across and patted his hand.

47.

Mrs B renews a friendship

The building was in a quiet back street, the other buildings in the street seemed to all be closed up.

"Can we take a walk around the back, do you think?" Mrs B opened the car door.

"No. I think we should wait for the police." He rested his hand on hers. "Please. You are too precious to me to let you put yourself in danger." He watched her face while she thought about what he had said.

"I understand that, but if Pamela is correct, someone is in grave danger in that building. The police will be here soon. I cannot be in too much danger just walking along a street." There was mischief in her smile.

"Well, I am coming with you." He gave in with good grace.

They walked together towards the back of the building. There was no sound or any sign that anyone was inside. A noise seemed loud in the silence, and Will turned to see what it was. Two young men stood by his car. He watched while one raised his foot and landed a heavy kick into the door. "Hey. Get away from there." The other raised a fist and Will set off at a fast pace. "Wait for me there." He called to Mrs B.

She watched him all the way back to the car, and the start of a heated discussion, before a door behind her opened, and she felt a pair of arms wrap around her and pull her inside. She let out a sharp cry and saw Will turn towards her before the door slammed shut.

"What on earth do you think you are doing?" She spluttered. The man next to her held his finger to his lips and then beckoned her to follow him. They stepped on the dusty floors and through a series of small rooms, they crossed one and then another, on tiptoe in the silence.

The man pointed through a slightly open door. "They have my wife." He whispered. "You offered to help her. She told me about you. Please, if you can do anything, now is the time."

Mrs B looked through the gap he had shown her. Maureen was tied to a chair, her head drooping low and blood on the part of her chin not hidden by her hair. "Oh, my." She turned to look at the man who had brought her there. "Why are you showing me this?"

"If I go in to get her, they will kill both of us. She said you were really clever. You found her when they couldn't. Please, can you help her?" He swallowed hard.

"Why did you distract Will away from me?" Her eyes narrowed.

"Who is Will?" His confusion seemed genuine.

"How many people are in there?" She nodded to the door.

"Two men in the next room. They are expecting more." A sound in the room next to them stopped their conversation.

Mr Bisley crossed the room into the area they could see. "Tell me where he is. This is your last chance, Maureen." He lifted her head, using her hair as a grip. He slapped her hard across the face. Mrs B watched the girl's head roll against her shoulder.

"Maybe she doesn't know, boss. We tried to get her to tell us before you got here." The man stepped forward, and Mrs B recognised him from the boxing gym.

"Maybe we just haven't asked the right question. Or the right way?" He reached for her chin and looked into her face. Her eyes seemed unfocused and confused. He raised his hand again, and she did not flinch.

"That's quite enough, Mr Bisley." Mrs B found herself stepping out of the shadows and into the room. "This young woman clearly has no idea where her husband is. I do know, and I can give you his address if you let her go." She moved closer to Maureen. "What a shameful way to behave. Pamela is such a lovely girl, I am surprised when you are capable of this sort of thing."

His eyebrows nearly hit his hairline. "What does that mean? You think I am stupid enough to let her go until I have her husband? Once I do, are you stupid enough to think I would let any of you go? Leave my daughter out of this."

"I'm not as silly as you think." Mrs B smiled. "You are a very powerful man, I know that, but sometimes, those you dismiss as being weak or, what was your word? Stupid? Yes. They are the ones that bring the most trouble to your door." Mrs B shook her head. "I am an annoying type of person. Mr Bisley, I am entirely aware of that. I am a busybody, interfering in the lives and interests of others."

"If you were to disappear, I suspect Pamela would fall into line and do as she was told." He leaned in close to her face. "Who knows, I might be able to rearrange the wedding before the end of the month?"

"Really?" The voice shocked both of them. Pamela stormed into the room, slamming the door behind her. "I won't marry Leonard. In fact, I have news, Daddy. I met someone, he's wonderful. We are planning a life together in another country. We will be somewhere you can't reach us."

"Pammie!" He reached for her. "You know I only want you to be happy."

"Then stop trying to make me do something that will make me miserable." She shrugged. "What the hell are you doing?" She spotted Maureen tied to the chair. "You seriously tied a girl to a chair and beat her up. I've never been so ashamed of you." Pamela crossed the room and started to work on the knots holding Maureen.

When the door burst open and Arnold arrived, Mrs B grabbed Pamela and pushed her into the room where Maureen's husband still hid. She worked on the knots that were still tied tightly around Maureen's wrists.

Arnold's men quickly subdued Mr Bisley's men, leaving Arnold to hold tight to their employer.

Will pushed through the door and found his way to her side, his eyes wide and his arms taking no time to wrap around her.

"Will, help me with these knots, my love." Together they worked at the rope, and released Maureen. Mrs B's fingers shook a little, but the warmth of Will's touch helped her.

"I need a statement from all of you." Mr Bisley glared at Arnold.

"I'll give you a statement." Pamela stepped out of

the shadows. "I know enough to keep you busy for the next few years. Sorry, dad, but it has to stop. I am going abroad, and I will be taking mum with me. You will be safely locked up. I wish you more than you wished me."

"How can you say that? You want to send me to prison?" He turned on her.

"I wish you what you deserve. You never wished that for me." She turned to Mrs B and fell into her arms.

"Oh, Mr Bisley?" He turned towards Mrs B as he was being led away. "I was not lying about Maureen's husband." He stepped out of the shadows and they all watched Mr Bisley's face grow red and his eyes widen.

"You were here! All that time, and you watched them beat your wife? What kind of man are you?" His eyes bulged from his face.

"He's weak, and foolish, and he ran up debts, but I think he is the man who Maureen loves. She knew he was here, and she could have given him up at any time, but she kept her mouth shut. You may not understand that kind of loyalty, but these two do." Mrs B watched Arnold lead Mr Bisley from the room and into the waiting car.

"You said you would help me." Maureen mumbled through her swollen lip.

"I did indeed, and I meant it too. I told you I was

tougher than you thought." Mrs B smiled across at Maureen. "Come along, dear. You need a cup of tea. That goes for you too, Pamela."

They walked out into the street, which was crowded with police officers. "Pamela? Say you didn't mean it. Please tell them that you won't give evidence against me."

"I am going to tell them everything that I can remember. Every crooked deal and sly backroom cheat that I know about. You have been getting away with this behaviour for so long, you think it's right." She stepped closer to the car. "You used to tell me that he who pays the piper calls the tune. I suspect that it's time to pay up." She stepped back from the car and raised her hand to wave.

"Who is the man you are planning a life with in a different country?" He sat forward, his hands cuffed behind his back.

"A doctor. His name is Gregory Williams." She watched him take in the information.

He sank back into the seats. "A doctor." There was a wistful quality to his voice. "Fancy that."

Arnold stepped between them. "I will need to take your statement, Miss Bisley. May I call by to speak to you later today?"

Her nod was curt, and she turned on her heel and walked away.

48.

Mrs B has a visit

"Mrs B? Hello?" Maisie stepped in through the back door.

"Maisie. Oh, my love. How wonderful to see you! Come in." Mrs B reached for Maisie's hands.

"I heard that you were planning a wedding, and I wondered if you might forget to invite us." Maisie smiled at her husband as he walked into the kitchen.

"Tommy! This calls for a cup of tea and biscuits." Mrs B fetched cups and settled herself at the table across from them. "Now, please tell me what you have been up to, and how you heard about the wedding. We haven't sent out invitations yet. Your names would have been at the top of the list."

"I am so looking forward to it." Tommy took a biscuit from the plate. "I hear that you and Arnold arrested Bisley." He shook his head. "You really are never going to stop putting yourself in danger, are you?"

"Good heavens, Tommy. I really do not do it on

purpose." She laughed.

"I hope Will knows what he's getting involved in." Tommy tapped his fingers on the table. The back door opened, and they all looked around to see Will standing there.

"Yes, thank you Tommy. I am absolutely aware, and very grateful." Will laughed. "I am very lucky to be marrying this lady." He sat down with a casual, gentle squeeze of his hand on hers.

"You are indeed, Will." Tommy kept his gaze level. "Did you ask Arnold to give you away?" Mrs B nodded. "Good, he's a nice man. I would have offered, but he's family."

"You are family too, Tommy." She shrugged. "I hope that you are both going to come to the wedding and dance the night away at the reception."

"We wouldn't miss it for the world." Maisie and Tommy reached across and took Mrs B's hands in theirs.

"Pamela should be home at any minute. I would very much like you to meet her. I think you will like her." Mrs B sipped from her cup. "She has had a very difficult time with her father, but we hope that this is all going to improve now that her father will be spending his time behind bars." Mrs B pushed the plate of biscuits across the table. "She really has been very brave."

"Are you ready for the big day?" Maisie leaned her chin on her hand. "It only seems a short time since we were running off to Scotland for our wedding."

"It is only a little while." Mrs B laughed.

"No, it's been months." Maisie rested her hand on the table, her rings glinting in the light. "I'm an old married lady now." She managed to keep a straight face for a few seconds, then collapsed against Tommy, both of them laughing together.

"We need to go, Maisie, if we are going to meet the parents for dinner." She nodded, and they both stood up. "The thing is, we have arranged a dinner tonight, with my dad, and Maisie's mum and dad, because we needed to have them all in one place, but we wanted to tell you first." Tommy cleared his throat. "We're expecting a baby. It's early days, so we are only telling family."

"Oh, my." Mrs B wrapped her arms around them both. "Thank you for trusting me. I am speechless. Wonderful news."

Will reached for Tommy's hands and shook, pulling his hand free to clap him on the back. "Congratulations to you both. I could not be happier for you."

"Just one thing." Tommy met Mrs B's eyes across the table. "Please don't tell our parents that you knew first."

"Perish the thought. Our lips are sealed." Mrs B watched the young couple climb into their car from the back door, with Will's arm wrapped tightly around her waist.

"Wonderful." Will leaned down and kissed Mrs B gently.

49.

Mrs B receives information

"I wanted to let you know what has been happening, and Barbara wanted to come and see you to organise things for the wedding. I hope that's alright?" Arnold sliced into the pork chop on his plate. "Delicious dinner, by the way."

"Bless you, I have always said that Mr Snelling at the butcher's in Little Melling is the best person to see if you want pork chops. Now, tell me what has happened." She pushed the gravy towards Arnold.

"Jimmy Malone was able to tell us a great deal, and even more, once we had Mr Bisley in custody. He has told us all about the night that Matthew Brunswick died, and who was there. Better than that, he confirmed that Mr Bisley paid them to go. We have a definite case against Mr Emerson and his sidekick, Billy Boy, for murder, and Mr Bisley too. Jimmy will be given a lighter sentence for his help and the other young boy who was taken along on that evening, has agreed with everything that Jimmy told us. We also have a case against Mr Bisley for extortion and kidnap, as well as grievous bodily harm against Maureen Stevens." Arnold took a breath and heaped up a forkful of dinner.

"You didn't tell Auntie the best thing." Barbara spooned some mashed potatoes and gravy into the baby's mouth. She watched her husband chew his mouthful. "He received a commendation from the Chief Superintendent and he's up for a promotion too. Honestly, Auntie, without your help, I am fairly sure that Mr Bisley would still be at large."

"What I would like to know is who wrote that music. That still rankles with me. I have a theory, but to be honest, finding out might be more trouble than not knowing." Mrs B chased a pea around her plate.

"Is there something that you need to tell me, Auntie?" Arnold turned towards her.

"No, not at all. I think this is not a police matter. Now, tell me, Barbara, what was it that you wanted to sort out for the wedding?" Mrs B steered the conversation towards her forthcoming nuptials.

"Oh, Auntie, I have found some wonderful ribbons to decorate your bouquet, and I had a chat with Maisie and Pamela. They both would very much like to be bridesmaids, and perhaps I thought we might choose from one of the fabric samples I have to make them both dresses. Also, we need to decide on whether or not to have the marquee up. It worked very well for Maisie and Tommy's wedding. We were lucky with the weather for ours, but you never know." She took a breath and popped another spoonful into the baby's mouth. "What do you think?"

"That sounds wonderful. I will ask Mrs Lennet." Mrs B listened to Barbara, but her mind also worked on her thoughts about the beautiful music she had found in Matthew Brunswick's flat.

50.

Mrs B and the musician

"I am so very sorry to bother you, Mr Phelps. Please, would you be able to spare me a few minutes?" Mrs B clutched the handle of her handbag in front of her body, as though it might act as a shield.

"Of course, Mrs B. Come on in." He held open the door and stepped backwards into the house.

"The weather has been rather wonderful this week, has it not? My garden is in dire need of watering." Mrs B looked out through the open French doors. "Your clematis is really rather lovely."

"Well, thank you, Mrs B. I am very fond of the blooms. My dear mother was wonderful with the flowers. I miss her." He turned back to her, his eyes a little misty. "Now, what can I do for you?"

"I wondered if you would play that music for me again?" Mrs B pulled the sheet music out of her handbag and passed it across to him. "I believe I know who wrote it, but I want to be sure. It is annoying me, like a loose thread on a jumper.

She watched while he sat at the piano, his eyes checking over the notes, settling himself.

His fingers ran over the keys, and the notes filled the room. The music was sweet, poignant. It reminded her of something that she had felt long before. She closed her eyes and breathed through the music. When it came to an end, she stayed exactly where she was.

"That was really rather wonderful." Mrs B rested her hand on the piano. "Thank you so much. You have a gift."

"You too, Mrs B." Mr Phelps watched her carry the sheet music out of the house.

He was waiting for her in the lane, visibly moved by the music and the conversation that he had heard through the window.

"I am so pleased that you found the time to meet me." She told him.

"Given your message, I really had very little choice." He fell into step with her, and together they walked up the hill.

51.

Mrs B makes a deal

"That piece of music was exceptional. When Mr Phelps played it, I closed my eyes, and I felt like I was six years old again. I was running across the meadow and down to the stream. The music took me there. You have a truly wonderful talent." Mrs B turned to look at him. The wooden bench she sat on was warm to the touch after a morning in the sunshine.

"Thank you. In fact, it forms part of a longer piece, but I have not completed it yet." He tugged a packet of cigarettes from his pocket. "What I do not understand is why this has to be a secret."

"I believe that having this amazing talent might prove fatal if details of it were to fall into the wrong hands." She blinked against the bright sunlight while she composed her thoughts and passed the sheet music to him. "You and I have not been the best of friends. When you first arrived, I thought that you might endanger Mrs Newton, or that your presence might ruin Maisie's wedding. I was wrong. The person in danger was always you."

"I really do not think that a piece of music could put me in danger. Whilst I am grateful for your concern, I think it is misplaced." He lit the cigarette that dangled from his lip. The end glowed in the flare of the flame from his lighter.

"Did you study music? Lessons?" Mrs B sat forward to see his reaction.

"No, I always played. My parents could not have afforded to pay for lessons." He shrugged.

"May I speak plainly?" Mrs B's brows pushed together, and she waited for his nod. "You had a relationship with Mrs Newton before she was married." She shifted her weight. "Her daughter was born just about nine months after she met Mr Newton. A convenient situation. However, Maisie has a talent for music, and she resembles you. That in itself is not enough. However, Mr Newton has always had a concern that Maisie might not be his daughter. If he were to put together the facts and see what I have seen, you would be in very grave danger."

"Oh." He swallowed hard. "What do you think I should do?"

"Well, that really rather depends." She took in a breath.

"On what?" He pulled the smoke deeply into his lungs and blew it out hard.

"Do you see a future with Mrs Newton? You

spoke about her as though she was merely a convenient stopping off point." Mrs B's words were clipped.

"No. You're right. She was a port in a storm, I suppose. Will you tell him? Newton, I mean?" The cigarette in his hand shook a little.

"I will make you a deal. I will keep your secret on one condition." He raised an eyebrow. "Maisie is very happy. She has a career, a husband, and she loves her parents. If you were to tell her that you are her father, it would unsettle her. If you are prepared to stay away, let her have her life, then I will keep your secret." She smiled across at him. "I will keep you safe."

"That is very reasonable." Mr Anderson stubbed out his cigarette. "Thank you, Mrs B. I have a couple of requests, though?"

"Of course." She waited for him to take a breath.

"Watch over her for me? I have always known. She told me that she was pregnant, but I was too stupid, too reckless to take responsibility. From time to time, I came back and watched from a distance. I knew Maisie was mine." He ran his hand through his hair.

"Naturally, I will watch over her. She is a very special girl. If she was not as dear to me as she is, I would not be here to ask for her to be allowed her life." Mrs B rested her hand on the warm wood of the bench between them.

"Would you give her this? You don't have to tell her it's from me, but I wrote it for her. I would like her to have it." He passed her the sheet music. His eyes brimmed with tears.

"I think you're wrong, you know." She patted his arm gently.

"I am?" He raised an eyebrow at her.

"You said you were not prepared to take the responsibility. I think you were, and you are. A little late, perhaps, but better late than never." Mrs B pushed herself up from the warm bench and walked away in the sunshine. "It looks as though it will be another lovely day." She crossed the lane and walked up the hill through the scent of summer blooms and freshly cut grass.

"Thank you, Mrs B." Mr Anderson's voice was quiet, glad to stay hidden from the danger, knowing that Maisie would be safe. Safer without him.

52.

Mrs B receives an insistent visitor

"Mrs B? Thank goodness that I have found you at home. We have several things that we need to discuss." Mrs Lennet came into the kitchen through the back door, and was followed in by Barbara.

"Hello. What a lovely surprise. I shall put on the kettle." Mrs B was indeed surprised when Barbara took the kettle from her hands.

"No, not at all. I will do that. You need to agree our suggestions. The lists are on the table." Barbara pointed and waited while Mrs B sat down to look at the lists that now covered her kitchen table.

"Well, what have we here? Food, decorations, flowers. I see. This is for Pamela's wedding to the young doctor." Mrs B caught Mrs Lennet shaking her head.

"This is the planning for your wedding. You have been so busy with saving everyone you meet, and solving every crime, we decided that if we did not make plans for your wedding, it would never happen. So please, tell us if we have done anything that you do not like. We are going ahead and booking the wedding we think you should have." Mrs Lennet leaned on the table. "It is all done. All you have to do is say yes. Or rather, I do."

Barbara brought tea to the table. "Please Auntie. Don't be offended. We just want you to have a life with Will. He loves you so much, but he won't pressure you to go ahead with the wedding. It has to be your choice."

"Offended? Perish the thought. Are you telling me that Will has been unhappy?" Mrs B caught a silent exchange between them.

"Not at all. He wants to marry you. But he wants you to choose him, not feel pressured. He loves you." Barbara held tightly to her hands.

"Well, I suspect I had better have the wedding sooner rather than later." She smiled across the table at them and watched their eyes lift to look at someone standing behind her.

"Wonderful news. Thank you, ladies. I am looking forward to the day." Will laughed at the shock on Mrs B's face when she turned to see him in the doorway.

"You knew about this?" Mrs B was almost indignant.

"Well, perhaps a little." He leaned against the

doorframe.

"Come on in and help us look through all these lists, then." Mrs B slid across into the next chair so that he could join them at the table.

"Oh, yes. I'm so glad there are going to be sausage rolls." Will ran his finger down the food list, looking content.

Barbara sipped her tea and watched the soon to be married couple share the decisions and the lists.

"Well, well, Mrs Lennet, it seems we will have a wedding." Barbara wrapped an arm around Mrs Lennet's shoulders.

"You're a wonderful planner, Barbara. Have you ever thought about joining the Village Fayre committee?" Mrs Lennet waited, hoping for a positive reply.

53.

Mrs B meets Mrs Bisley

Pamela knocked on the kitchen door and let herself in. "Mrs B? Are you at home?"

"Pamela? Hello dear. How lovely." Mrs B came through into the kitchen. "Ah hello, you must be Pamela's mother. She looks so like you."

"Mrs B? It is an absolute honour. I owe you such a huge debt of gratitude. Pamela's freedom from my husband is more than I could have wished for." She reached for Mrs B's hands and shook them in her own.

"Oh my, it was my pleasure. You have a wonderful daughter. She is an absolute joy. I hear that you are going abroad with Pamela and her soon to be husband." Mrs B filled the kettle, and offered her two visitors a chair at the table.

"I will be joining them later. But I have some things to sort out here first, and I think the last thing they need is me in the way on their honeymoon." She laughed gently.

"Have you heard from your father, Pamela?" Mrs B put cups of tea in front of both of them, and received a shake of the head in answer from Pamela. "The reason I ask is that I have. I had a letter from him requesting that I visit him. If I am completely honest, it has come as something of a shock."

"Will you go?" Pamela paused with her cup of tea midway between the table and her lips.

"I have not decided. The letter only arrived this morning. I shall let you know once I have thought about it, and talked to Will." She smiled. "Now, tell me about the wedding? I am so excited to see you married to Gregory. The only thing that has been a surprise is how quickly you have decided to marry." Mrs B looked carefully into her teacup, as though the answer might be hiding there.

"You knew? Oh, my goodness, am I ever going to get anything past you?" Pamela laughed.

"Perish the thought. I did not know. I did wonder." Mrs B reached across the table and patted Pamela's hand.

"I have known Gregory for two years. We met when I was at school. He was in medical school then." She took a breath. "I could never have married Leonard. He was so exceedingly dull, but I was already in love with Gregory. When you told me that you lived in Little Mellington, I could not believe my luck. Gregory had already given in his notice and accepted the job abroad. I was planning to stay out of sight working in the nightclub for a while, but then Matt was killed and it was all such a mess." Pamela smiled. "Then I met my guardian angel. You have made my life so easy and wonderful. I know you put yourself at risk to help me, and I will be grateful forever."

Mrs B stood on her back doorstep and waved Pamela and her mother off. There was something unsettling about Mrs Bisley. Perhaps she had spent so much time with dangerous people, some of that danger had rubbed off. Whatever it was, Mrs B was worried.

54.

Mrs B does some research

"Mr Newton? Hello, is Mr Newton at home?" The burly man looked at Mrs B carefully.

"You're Mrs B, aren't you? We all heard what happened. It has to be exaggerated, but you are a legend." He smiled nervously. "I'll find Mr Newton. Perhaps you might like to have a seat?"

"Thank you very much." Slightly bemused, she sat down and waited for Mr Newton to appear. She did not have long to wait.

"Mrs B? Good to see you. I heard your news, and I suspect you heard mine, too." He pulled up a chair and joined her at the table.

"I heard that you are to be a grandfather, which is really rather wonderful. Congratulations. I plan to call in on Mrs Newton to offer my congratulations to her on the way home." She laid her hands on the table. "There is another matter which I need to discuss with you. I am in need of advice."

"Is it likely that you will take any advice from me?" He tipped his head on one side.

"I will not know until I have heard it." She smiled.

"Fair enough. Tell me how I can help." He sat back and waited.

"I am sure that you have heard about Mr Bisley. I wanted to ask two questions." He nodded for her to continue. "Mrs Bisley. I met her, and I had a feeling that she was perhaps not as honest as she might be?"

"Oh, now. You are asking. I would have to tell you a great many things which I am not permitted to tell you to explain this." He stood, pacing across the room and back again. "Right. I can tell you that you are right. She is not the downtrodden wife that she makes herself out to be. She comes from a complicated family. Your instinct with regard to this one is correct. I do not believe that she would harm her daughter, or you. However. It seems that Mr Bisley may have misbehaved, and become less useful to her, or perhaps he just outlived his usefulness." He took a breath. His face working through the decisions in front of her. "If I may suggest?" Mrs B nodded her agreement. "Stay out of her way. If, as I hear it, her daughter is to leave the country, wave goodbye and stay away from the mother."

"Thank you, Mr Newton. I know that I am asking a great deal. Can you tell me if Pamela is aware of her mother's dishonesty?" Mrs B took a breath and waited.

"No, I would think probably not. It's possible, but they sent her away to school, so that she was not involved. My guess would be no." He watched her think about what she had been told.

"Thank you, Mr Newton. You have been most helpful. I made a fresh batch of biscuits this morning. Would you like some?"

"I would. Very much. Thank you, Mrs B." He smiled as she stood up, perhaps grateful that there were no more questions.

She pulled a greaseproof paper parcel from her handbag and placed it on the table in front of him. "I am certain that you will be a very good grandfather, Mr Newton. My congratulations again."

Mrs B smiled widely at the young man standing by the door and thought about what she had learned while she waited for the bus.

55.

Mrs B receives a warning

Mrs B was in the middle of laying out thinly sliced ham on plates for dinner. The salad leaves and tomatoes were waiting for her on the table. Dinner would be ready when Will arrived.

When a knock on the back door interrupted her, she opened the door, surprised to find Mrs Bisley on the step.

"Mrs Bisley? This is a surprise." Mrs B wiped her hands on the tea cloth tucked into the waistband of her apron. "Can I help?"

"Yes. I need a quick word." The woman waited for an invitation into the kitchen and stepped inside when she received one.

Mrs B moved the plates and the salad from the table.

"I won't keep you long. You and I have a great deal in common. The way that you have helped Pamela is very kind and appreciated." She smiled across the table.

"My pleasure. She's a lovely girl." Mrs B tipped her

head to one side.

"Your efforts to remove my husband were, as it turned out, convenient for me. He is better off out of my way, and his absence suits my purposes for the moment." Mrs Bisley leaned on the table. "Do not confuse me with Mrs Newton. She was always a plus one. I have always been the senior partner in my relationship." She watched Mrs B carefully. "You're clever. I see past this flowered apron nonsense, but do not make the mistake of thinking that I will allow you to interfere in my business."

"Well, well, Mrs Bisley. This flowery apron is to protect my dress from whatever I am cooking. I protected Pamela from your husband. Whilst I understand that she is a very astute young woman, I presume that she is unaware of your involvement in the family business." Mrs B laid her hands on the table. "You are very kind to come and tell me about your position, but I cannot see how it would affect me."

"Don't play me for a fool. I know that you have been asking around about me. You're an annoying busybody, and nothing good ever happens to those sorts of people." Mrs Bisley leaned across the table. "Do you like olives, Mrs B?"

"I do not believe that I have ever tasted one." Mrs B was wrongfooted by the sudden change in the direction of the conversation.

"That's the point. I have worked hard for years to give my daughter a wonderful life. She went to good schools. Before she could say it, she knew she enjoyed foie gras, she liked olives. Somebody wiser than I am told me that those are acquired tastes, but first you must acquire the foie gras and the olives. Do you understand? My daughter has been brought up with expectations, and I will not allow you to thwart them." Her breathing was a little laboured.

"Perish the thought that I would imagine you to be foolish. I do, however, imagine you to be a loving mother. We are on the same side as far as Pamela is concerned. I think we both want her to start a new, clean life with Gregory, do we not?" Mrs B raised an eyebrow. "We would like her to leave without finding out who will be running the business as well."

"You would be well advised to keep me on your side. I am not a good enemy to have." Mrs Bisley pushed her chair back with a scrape on the floor. "I hear that you are to be married. So many people that you love. Accidents happen. It would be such a shame."

"Mrs Bisley, I think we have something else in common." Mrs B smiled and nodded. "You are also a Mrs B, are you not? Neither of us are the clothes we wear. You are not your sharp suits or your expensive hats anymore than I am my flowered apron. We can perhaps agree to a period of calm while we wait for Pamela to leave for her new life. I make no promises after that." Mrs B watched and waited for Mrs Bisley to react.

"Very well. We will hide behind our smiles until then, but remember my warning. Stay out of my way." Mrs Bisley stood up and let herself out of the back door. Her heels tip-tapping on the garden path.

Mrs B collected the salad she was making and continued to load the plates. If her hand shook a little, it was hardly surprising.

56.

Mrs B is surprised

"Well, my kitchen is busier than Piccadilly Circus today. Come on in Reverend Chambers. How can I help?" Mrs B's cup of tea was half finished. "There's another cup in the pot if you would like one?"

"Thank you, Mrs B. I think I would. This is all very much irregular." He slumped into the chair and accepted the cup once it was poured.

"Whatever has happened?" Mrs B was concerned to see him so perturbed.

"I have married couples on a special licence before, Mrs B, but not with quite so much skulduggery. I am commissioned by the young couple to request your attendance at the church and not to give you their names. Your fiancé is also invited." He took another sip. "I am not certain that this comes under my official remit.

"Hello Reverend Chambers. I am sorry, I didn't hear you come in." Will came into the kitchen.

"We are invited to a wedding. To be carried out on a special licence, and apparently we are not to know the names of those involved." Mrs B turned to Will. "Would you like to go?"

"When is the wedding?" Will leaned against the door frame.

"Now." Reverend Chambers checked his watch. "In two minutes."

"We shall have no time to change. Well, we shall have to go as we are then. We had better hurry." Mrs B laughed. "What fun!"

"Do not worry, Mrs B. They really cannot start without me." They walked down the lane together and arrived at a very quiet church.

"Is anyone here?" Mrs B reached for Will's hand.

"Yes. I believe the happy couple are inside." Reverend Chambers opened the door.

"Mrs B! Will! You came. Thank you so much." Pamela threw her arms around them both.

"Pamela? This is your wedding?" Mrs B looked up the aisle to see Gregory waiting, transferring his weight from one foot to the other nervously.

"Yes, isn't it a hoot?" Pamela's eyes sparkled with excitement. "I wondered if you would be Gregory's best man, Will, and you might give me away, Mrs B?"

"What will your mother say? She would want to be here for your wedding." Mrs B was more than a little shocked.

"She'll be furious, but we will be far away by then." Pamela laughed.

"If you are ready?" Reverend Chambers stood waiting at the altar.

Will walked up the aisle and shook hands with Gregory. They turned towards Mrs B and Pamela.

"If you're certain, this is what you want." Mrs B held Pamela's hands.

"Absolutely. Mum thinks I don't know what's been going on. I've known for years. I just want to get away from both of them. She won't know where I am. Please, Mrs B." Pamela reached for Mrs B's shoulders. "I just want to start again without all their nonsense in the background."

"Very well. Congratulations." Mrs B held out her elbow for Pamela to slip her hand through. "Here we go."

Half an hour later, after embracing Mrs B and Will, Gregory started the car, and Pamela ran to the passenger side. The back seat was piled with suitcases, and the happy couple smiled through the window. The ink was barely dry on the marriage certificate, but certainly they were married.

In the warmth of the summer evening, Mrs B and Will stood with Reverend Chambers and waved until the car had disappeared out of the village.

"You two will be next. I am looking forward

to that ceremony." Reverend Chambers clapped Will on the back. "I hope the new doctor starts soon. We seem to spend half our time in the surgery with one thing or another."

Will held Mrs B's hand as they walked up the hill. "I suspect her mother will be furious."

"You may be right. However, Pamela gave me some paperwork before she climbed into the car, which might be of interest to Arnold. Perhaps her mother might have other things to worry about." She smiled up at him as they reached her garden gate. "Those tomatoes were nice in the salad tonight, weren't they?"

"Yes, they were. From your garden?" She nodded. "Delicious." He leaned down to kiss her cheek.

"All that for a tomato?" She laughed.

"I wasn't talking about the tomato." He held the gate open and they walked through the garden in the evening sunshine.

57.

Mrs B has a difficult conversation.

The house was certainly imposing. Will had driven her there. He had insisted, and although she considered his behaviour to be overprotective when she looked up at the enormous building in front of her, she was very pleased that he was there.

"I will see you in a little while. Thank you for trusting me, Will." She reached across and kissed him tenderly.

"Don't be too long. I need to talk to you about something later." He smiled and watched her climb out of the car.

The front door was double the height of her back door. She reached for the bell and heard the answering tone within the house. The sound of steps behind the door made her stand a little straighter.

"Mrs B? Well, I am surprised. You had better come in." Mrs Bisley stood back and opened the door.

Inside, the house seemed even bigger. "Well, Mrs

Bisley, this is certainly an impressive house." Mrs B looked up the stairs and imagined Pamela there as a child. Had she enjoyed playing in the dark wood panelled hallway?

"Yes. It is the house I always wanted. When I was a child, my mother worked here. She sweated in the kitchens, cooking for the people who lived here. I knew I could be something much more than my parents were. We are not so very different. You're clever, but you would not be accepted as a police officer, would you? I had to find a man to stand in front of me, be the public face of my business. In just the same way as you solve the crimes and then pass the information to your puppy of a nephew." She led the way into an enormous living room and poured two drinks. She passed one to Mrs B, who waited until Mrs Bisley has turned away to sniff it dubiously.

"Thank you." Mrs B sipped. "Oh."

"It's whiskey. Perhaps you think it's a man's drink. But you and I are the men in our lives, aren't we?" Mrs Bisley sipped her drink. "Tell me about my daughter's wedding."

"She had arranged it all, and we received a message, through the vicar, asking us to attend. The only people there were the bride and groom and Will and myself." Mrs B watched Mrs Bisley's face.

"She knew, didn't she?" She waited for Mrs B's

nod. "After everything I did. It was all for her. To give her a better life." She sipped again.

"Well, you did. She is with a man she loves, and starting a new and exciting life. She has a better life." Mrs B sipped again, her eyes wide with the strength of the drink. "You told me that she had tasted foie gras and enjoyed it before she could pronounce it. Honestly, I think what you gave her was a taste for an honest life, and she has gone to get it. You have achieved what you set out to do." Mrs B set her glass down carefully. "I imagine it's lonely up here in this big house, but you can console yourself with the fact that your daughter will be happy."

"So, what brings you here today? I cannot imagine that you came to chat without some agenda." Mrs Bisley sat on a sofa across from Mrs B.

"Of course. Enough chit chat. Pamela gave me some papers when she left, with instructions to pass them on to my....puppy of a nephew." Mrs B took a breath. "Obviously, I did as I was asked."

Mrs Bisley's brows pushed together. "What sort of papers?"

"Pamela was fully aware of your role in the family business, and she had collected proof. I imagine that it took her some years to gather it all. In any case, it seems that it was really quite incriminating for you and for your husband."

Mrs B reached her hands out to Mrs Bisley.

"Did she hate me so much?" Mrs Bisley wiped a finger under her eye.

"No, I think she hated your choices. Perhaps she wanted to set everything right. Honestly, I cannot answer for her motivation." Mrs B stood up. "We should go."

"Go?" Mrs Bisley was wrongfooted. "We are not going anywhere."

"We have an appointment." Mrs B led Mrs Bisley to the front door.

"Did she tell you where they will be living?" Mrs Bisley turned to face Mrs B.

"No. She told me she was telling nobody." Mrs B reached for the lock on the front door.

"I will miss her." Mrs Bisley turned to Mrs B. "She will be in touch with you. Will you tell her that I love her?"

"Of course. I think you will find that she already knows." Mrs B opened the door. Arnold was standing on the doorstep.

"Mrs Bisley? I need you to accompany me to the police station." Arnold stepped back.

"And if I do not wish to?" Mrs Bisley bristled.

"In that case, I have sufficient evidence to arrest you. My aunt asked that she might be able to make this easier for you. She thought that you deserved that. Please don't prove her wrong." Arnold reached for her arm.

"Not so much of a puppy as I thought." Mrs Bisley laughed. "Thank you, Mrs B."

58.

Mrs B makes a visit

"Take a look through those brochures while I drive. I thought we might be able to get away for a week, or maybe two, after the wedding. Perhaps we could spend some time on our own, just for once." Will smiled across at her.

"I'm sorry, Will. I know my life is a little full." She picked up one of the brochures. "This looks pretty."

"Wherever you want to go. I will be happy to go with you." He reached across to hold her hand. They pulled up outside the prison. "Are you sure you want to go through with this?"

"Thank you, Will. I'll be fine. Thank you for driving me." She reached across and kissed him.

The gates clanged closed behind her, and despite the fact that she had been expecting it, it jarred her enough to make her jump. The officer opened the next gate, and she walked through, along with the other visitors.

The visitors took a seat and waited for the gate at the other end of the room to open. The women around her, and they were all women, had an altogether tougher look about them than she did, she knew. They stood, accustomed to the feeling of being part of the herd. Mrs B bristled at the thought and stood up a little straighter than before.

The next gate opened, and they filed into a room filled with small tables. The guard took a piece of paper from each woman and told her which table to sit at. It was a slow process, but eventually Mrs B handed her slip of paper to him and was directed to sit down. When everyone was seated, the gate they had come through was closed and another one, on the other side of the room opened, allowing prisoners in.

Mr Bisley looked smaller in his prison uniform than he had in his own clothes.

"You came to see me. Thank you. I wasn't sure that you would." He sat down and rested his hands on the table.

"I wasn't sure that I would either. But you asked me to, and as we are not friends, I presumed that you had something of importance to discuss." She tipped her head to the side and waited.

"Yes. Of course. The thing is, that I have lived a life filled with pretence. When you live like that, you become good at spotting others who are pretending, and those who have no pretending at all in their lives." He nodded his head. "You have a strong sense of what is right and what is wrong. I see that for certain. You took care of my daughter when she was in danger, and for that, I am grateful. Not so pleased about your arranging for me to move to my present home, but we win and we lose, I suppose." He smiled, but there was little joy in it.

"I understand, I think. Perhaps if I told you that Pamela is married to her young doctor, and they have left to live a life abroad, would that give you some peace?" Mrs B's eyebrows pushed closer together.

"You were there, at the wedding?" His face changed entirely.

"Yes, indeed, I was. She was a beautiful bride, and truly happy." Mrs B smiled across at him. "It may be difficult to know that she married without you being there, but I can promise you that she has left with a happy and joyful future ahead of her."

"Was her mother there?" He leaned forward to hear the answer.

"No. Pamela decided not to invite her." Mrs B kept her voice low.

"Wonderful news!" He threw his head back and laughed. "She finally got out from under. I could not be more proud of her." He rocked from side to side with his laughter. "I only put in a not guilty plea so that I could see her again. The one true joy in my whole life. If she is happy and ready to start a new life as a doctor's wife, then I shall change my plea to guilty." He heard Mrs B's sharp intake of breath. "I know it will mean the hangman's noose for me, but I will die happy in the knowledge that she is safe and away from her mother."

"You astound me, Mr Bisley. You presented a very different personality when I met you last." Mrs B peered across at him as though seeing him for the first time.

"Oh, you have no idea, Mrs B. Do you really have any interest in finding out? I wonder?" He shot her another wide smile.

"Now you have my interest." Mrs B sat forward a little.

"Have you met my wife?" His sudden change of direction wrong footed Mrs B.

"I have indeed. Pamela introduced us." Mrs B kept her eyes on the table, not sure what his reaction would be to knowing that his wife was currently awaiting trial.

"Will Pamela give evidence against her as well?" The urgency in his voice made Mrs B sit up straight and meet his stare.

"Yes. She will." She nodded emphatically.

"Then the circle is complete. I am so grateful." He sat back from the table. "If you wish to investigate, and it may be that you do not, then you should start with Charlie Hemsworth at the Oxford Playhouse." He pushed himself to his feet. "Thank you for coming to see me. I suspect we shan't meet again." He turned away. "If you hear from Pammie, tell her…tell her that she'll always be my best girl."

He walked away, towards the gate, his shoulders stooped as though under a heavy burden, while Mrs B sat at the table, wiping her eyes and trying to pull herself together.

59.

Mrs B goes in search of Mr Hemsworth

"How did it go?" Will welcomed her back to the car with a hug.

"I really am at a loss to answer you." Mrs B sat back into the seat. "I wonder if he is sending me on a wild goose chase. But I know I will not be able to resist an investigation like this until it is resolved." She laughed.

"Could we start from the beginning?" Will started the engine. "Are we going home?"

"I rather think we should go to the Oxford Playhouse, and I can tell you what happened on the way." She turned towards him. "Is that alright with you?"

"I would go to the top of Mount Everest if you would go with me." He smiled and started the engine.

"Thank you Will. I don't deserve you." She reached for his hand.

"Of course you do. Now tell me what happened." He squeezed her fingers.

He listened intently to what she had heard. It took nearly an hour by the time he had asked all the questions he wanted to. She had tried to keep her answers exact, and to explain carefully when Will asked for more.

The playhouse was a smartly painted building in the famous university town. The doors were closed and locked against their efforts, but the alley around the side of the building led them to the stage door, which was open, not wide open, but there was enough of a gap for Will to slide his hand in and pull the door wide enough for them to slip through.

On the stage, a rehearsal was underway. A strong male voice lifted through the theatre and Mrs B stood still to listen.

"What a wonderful voice. I wonder if that is who we are looking for." She turned to look at Will, who shrugged and stepped a little closer to the side of the stage.

Mrs B stood behind him and listened to the song finish. Several voices broke the silence, which dropped at the end of the singing. The voices quietened again, and the piano notes rang out. The voice that lifted through the dust motes was more familiar to Mrs B than the back of her own hand. "Maisie!" She whispered. "That's Maisie."

"Mrs B?" Tommy stepped out of the shadows. "How did you know we were here?"

"Tommy! I really didn't. But I am so glad that you are." Mrs B reached for Tommy and he leaned down to kiss her cheek, before reaching to shake Will's hand.

"I am looking for someone. Perhaps you can help. Do you know Charlie Hemsworth?" Mrs B caught the surprised expression on Tommy's face.

"Yes, of course. I will take you to meet him, but say hello to Maisie first. She would be so upset if you don't." He held his finger to his lips and led them silently behind the stage. The need for quiet meant that the questions about Charlie Hemsworth that Mrs B wanted to ask, would have to wait.

60.

Mrs B and an introduction

Will and Mrs B followed Tommy through the curtains and joined him at the side of the stage, where they could watch Maisie fill the theatre with notes that were so strong, floating on the emotion she gave them, that nobody in the building was moving. They stood still in awe of the clarity of her voice.

When the last note drifted to a close, she turned on her heel and spotted Mrs B. "Oh what a lovely surprise" She crossed the space between them. "So lovely to see you." She hugged hard and stepped back to wipe her eyes.

"Thank you, Maisie. It's looking like it will be a good show tonight." The man crossed the stage, checking his clipboard. "Where is the juggler?"

"Thanks Charlie." Maisie turned back to Will and Mrs B.

"Mr Hemsworth?" Mrs B stepped forward. The man with the clipboard turned towards her.

"Hello?" His patchy moustache twitched along with his lip.

"I wonder if I might have a word once you have a moment?" Mrs B raised an eyebrow.

"About?" His one word gave a guarded impression.

"Mr Bisley gave me your name. He seemed to think that you might be able to tell me a little about him." She heard Tommy's sharp intake of breath, but ignored it.

"Bisley? There's name I haven't heard for a while. Yes, alright, he was a decent bloke, for an actor. Most of them are a bundle of nerves or so full of themselves they look like they might pop. Give me ten minutes to finish the run through, and I'll sit down with you." He nodded and walked back to the centre of the stage. "Juggler? Where is the juggler?" A young man with a suitcase ran onto the stage. "Are you the juggler? If you're late tonight, you're out of a job. Do you hear?"

In the end, it was closer to twenty minutes before Charlie Hemsworth brought his clipboard to his chest and came to find Mrs B, where she was sitting with Will and Tommy. Maisie had made her excuses and gone to have a rest before her performance that evening.

"Right. Sorry to keep you waiting. What did you want to know?" Mr Hemsworth sat down and rested the clipboard on his knees.

"I would very much like to hear what you remember about Mr Bisley." Mrs B leaned towards him.

"Ok. He worked here. I think he must have been here six months. He was young, of course, but he had a way about him. There was something believable about him." He smiled. Clearly, these were fond memories. "This was a while ago, before the war. We expected young actors to know every part and step in where they were needed. He never let me down. Best part he ever played was as a gangster. He was a very affable fellow, but that night I was afraid of him." He nodded. "That was the last week he was here, I think. Or if not, it was soon after that."

"Did he have a girlfriend? Someone serious?" Mrs B tipped her head to the side.

"Not that I remember. But maybe I wouldn't. Oh, there was a girl. Pretty little thing. Only in the last week or two, I think. Her name was Amanda, no Anthea, no, that's not right either. Something like that." A shout from the back of the stage took his attention. "Sorry, I have to go. Maisie's a wonder, but with the rest of them, it's like herding cats." He rushed back up onto the stage and disappeared through the curtains.

"What on earth have you got involved in now?" Tommy leaned on the back of the seats between Will and Mrs B.

"I think we really need to find out. It has been lovely to see you, Tommy. Give Maisie a kiss for us." Mrs B held his shoulders and kissed his cheek.

"Be careful of the Bisley family. He's dangerous, but she's lethal." He wrapped his arms around Mrs B. "I've missed you and all of your investigating."

Will shook Tommy's hand and guided Mrs B through the stage door. "Right, so where do we need to go now?"

"Home, I think. We need to feed Marmalade and decide what this means. I suspect we should have something to eat, too."

61.

Mrs B goes in search of the mask

Arnold knocked on the back door. "Auntie? Are you at home?"

"Arnold, how lovely. What a nice surprise." She reached for him and he kissed her cheek.

"Not such a nice one, perhaps. I have received a letter from Pamela. The evidence she gave us against her mother is watertight, but we have been going through what she gave us on her father, and unless she provides a witness statement, we have nothing that justifies keeping him locked up." He accepted the cup of tea that she passed him. "Thank you, Auntie. Did she leave you an address?"

"No. I have no address." She slid into a chair at the table. "I have been doing a little investigating, and I think perhaps Pamela did that on purpose."

"Oh?" Arnold helped himself to a biscuit.

"It seems that Mr Bisley was a jobbing actor as a young man, and really quite talented, from what I have heard. I think it is possible that Mrs Bisley married him because he could play the part quite effectively, but she was always the driving power. She ran the business and made the decisions, using him as a shield. I am wondering if Pamela maybe knew that all along, and planned it this way." She caught Arnold's confused expression. "I am not saying that I understand why she would help us to arrest her father. I wish she was here so that I could ask her."

"You saw him hit Maureen, though, didn't you?" Arnold sipped from his cup.

"His back was to me." She closed her eyes to check the picture in her memory. "I saw him raise his arm and bring it down, but no, I did not see him actually hit her. I believed that he did." She took a breath. "What about Maureen? She could tell you who hit her."

"She could if she had not disappeared. I can't make any of the charges work." He shook his head.

"I wonder. Could Pamela have planned all of this? She gave me the address of the warehouse, and Maureen was the only one who told me that her husband was in danger from Mr Bisley. Why was Matthew Brunswick killed, though? Oh, my goodness, I think I may have been absolutely and entirely stupid. We need to get to the nightclub right now, unless we are already too late." Mrs B pushed her feet into her shoes.

Arnold parked the car in the street outside the

nightclub and together they pushed the front doors, but found them closed. The alley she had pulled Pamela through took them to the door into the kitchen, which stood open. "Come on, Arnold."

"Can you please tell me exactly what has happened?" Arnold followed in her wake.

"What has been happening, I believe, is that we have been shown a play. Actors following a script. Hurry now." She climbed the stairs towards the back of the building with Arnold only two steps behind. The office door was closed, and Mrs B did not pause to knock. "Mr Peters, I am so very glad that I caught you."

"You? For heaven's sake. I answered all your questions. I am a busy man, so if you want to talk to me, you need to make an appointment." He busied himself with the paperwork.

"I think you had a short affair with Maureen. That was the only truth that you told us when we spoke last. Other than that, it was all lies, wasn't it?" Mrs B perched on the edge of the only unoccupied chair in the room.

"You are an annoying old woman. I have told you no lies at all. You really can't come in here accusing people." His hands spread on the papers on his desk.

"I am annoying. I agree. Could you take a look at those papers on his desk, Arnold? The way he is trying to cover them up suggests that you might find something of interest there." Arnold reached across and held Mr Peters' hand on the desk.

"It's a staff rota." Arnold's eyebrows push together.

"Yes, what's the date?" Mrs B shook her head at her nephew. "The day that Matthew Brunswick was murdered. The boys from the gym told the truth. They did beat him up, but they left him in his flat, probably unconscious. Mr Peters here arrived later, and used the gloves with the glass in them, to kill a defenceless man." She shook her head. "Then he put the gloves in the rubbish bin outside the gym for us to find."

"Why would I do it? Matt was a good doorman. The only one I could rely on if there was trouble." He shrugged.

"May I look at the rota?" Mrs B held her hand out and Arnold passed it to her. She ran her finger down the list. "Oh. Matthew was working that night. Check the other piece of paper he was trying to hide. Please, Arnold." She turned the paper over. "Oh, well, here's a thing." She smiled. "I recognise this handwriting." She showed the paper to Arnold. "Matthew was doing a stock take on that day, was he not, Mr Peters?"

"Here's something else. Oh yes, this is interesting too." He passed her another sheet.

"Oh dear, Mr Peters. It seems that Matthew wrote you a note on the back of the staff rota. It says: 'There is more stock than there should be. What is going on?' But you knew that, didn't you, Mr Peters?" She turned the paper around and showed it to Mr Peters. "The other piece of paper is a note from your employer, wanting to know why the takings are going down." She nodded slowly. "I believe I could explain it. You were buying stolen alcohol and putting it through the bars. You were taking the profit on it. I think Matthew found out when he checked the stock. Your employer would not have taken too kindly to your behaviour, I believe."

"You have no proof." He laughed, but the sound was empty of anything except bravado.

"I think we actually do." Arnold leaned against the door frame. "The papers from Matthew's flat that made no sense. Lists of numbers and initials. We had no idea what it meant, but now that you say he checked the stock, I remember the two columns of figures."

"Also, we know who owns this club. Your employer would not just fire you for the theft. Your life would be in danger." Mrs B watched him think about it.

"Fine. Yes. I put a few crates of whiskey through the bar. I needed the money. Matt was being a self-righteous idiot. When the thugs from the gym turned up, it was like a gift. But I didn't kill him. I didn't stop them either." He shrugged. "I'll pay back the money from the whiskey, no problem."

"I think we need to continue this conversation at the police station. Mr Peters, please come with me." Arnold steered Mr Peters out of the room.

Mrs B leaned across the desk and took a look at the papers Mr Peters had pushed onto the floor. "Wonderful." She told the empty room. "I am certain that this will be useful." The paper in her hand had Matthew Bruswick's distinctive scrawl on it. It said I think it's BIG. The stocktake is all wrong.

62.

Mrs B has a surprise visitor

Mrs B was just about ready to go to see Mrs Pendle. She had fetched her coat and laid it over the back of her kitchen chair when someone knocked at the door.

"Hello?" Mrs B pulled the door open.

"You came to visit me. I wanted to return the favour." His voice was entirely different. Mr Bisley no longer growled like a gangster.

"Who are you playing now?" Mrs B tipped her head to one side. "You sound very friendly. Is that an act, too?"

"If I am to be honest, I've forgotten who I used to be, so I am trying on some characters. I quite like this one." He smiled, and she wondered if there was a purpose for his visit. "I'm here because I wanted to thank you. Pamela was certain that you would spot all the clues." He raised his eyebrow.

"Come on in. I'll put the kettle on. I think you have something to tell me." Mrs B stood back and waited for him to make himself comfortable at the kitchen table. She filled the kettle and sat down with him.

"Pamela has a real talent for the theatre. She used to be in plays at school. She was entirely wonderful. Such a clever little girl, too. She always knew, you know." He watched her get up and make the tea. "Not all of it was pretend. She was truly very attached to you."

"She gave me the address of the warehouse. After telling me all the stories about how scary you were." Mrs B passed him a cup of tea. "You were very believable. When I came to see you at the golf club, you worried me a great deal." She sipped her cup of tea.

"Yes, she set up the whole thing. She did lie about one thing, though. I wanted to let you know before you found out." He took a sip from his cup. "Good tea." He put the cup down carefully. "Gregory didn't get a job abroad. They just went away for a little while. A honeymoon, I suppose. So, they will be back soon, and my little Pammie will be the local doctor's wife."

"Oh. Well, I suppose I will be very glad to have the doctor we all know and trust back working in the village." She sat back. "I will be very glad to see Pamela again. She is a very resourceful, if slightly underhanded, young lady, and I think Mrs Lennet has a dress for her to try on, if she still intends to be a bridesmaid at my wedding."

Mrs B pulled a tin across the table and prised off the lid. "Have a biscuit, Mr Bisley."

"Oh, the famous biscuits. I heard about these from a good friend." He took one and bit into it. "Oh, every bit as wonderful as I have been led to believe."

"I think you are a good deal nicer than I had been led to believe, Mr Bisley." Mrs B pushed the biscuit tin closer to him and smiled when he helped himself to another.

"I think this new character is one that likes biscuits much more than any I have ever played." His eyes crinkled at the sides and he chuckled to himself.

63.

Mrs B and Will make decisions

"I need to talk to you. I've made tea and got out the biscuits. There's nothing left for you to do except have a conversation with me." Will waited for her to sit down at the kitchen table with him. "Good. Now I will pour the tea and you can drink it while I talk."

"Are you cross?" Mrs B's brows pushed together.

"No. I am a little concerned." He pushed a cup across the table to her and she smiled. "The last few weeks have been very busy. We have been all over the place investigating this thing with Pamela's parents, and it made me think." He pushed the plate of biscuits to her. "If I was busy, you would have gone alone, wouldn't you?"

"Yes. Of course." She took a sip.

"Now that I am no longer working for the police, I need to find some gainful employment. I also need to keep you from walking into a dangerous situation on your own. I have come up with an idea, which I think is rather ingenious, which would solve both problems in one go." He smiled and raised his eyebrows.

"What is it, Will?" She smiled. "You do look very pleased with yourself."

"I propose that we set up a private investigation agency. Equal partners, just as we always have been, and I hope we always will be. The police have a budget to pay for outside assistance, and people might hire us to look for missing relatives or to help a family member who has been wrongfully accused of a crime. That way, we would earn some money, and you and I could be together." He sat back and took a biscuit.

"What about my cleaning jobs? Could I still do that?" She rested her hands on the table. "I would not want to let down people who have been my customers for a long time."

"Of course. I should think we would not be particularly busy to start with." He reached for her hands. "Unless you think I am interfering."

"I think it would be very exciting. But perhaps we would not charge people very much, and charge the police more?" She laughed, watching his face change from delighted to surprised and back again.

"Yes. We would have to decide as we went along, I suppose. But you agree to the idea in principle?" He held tightly to her hands.

"Yes, I do. I think it's a wonderful idea. I shall let

Arnold know, so that he can tell the police that they should expect to pay from now on, and that they will be getting an ex-Chief Inspector for the price as well!" She raised her cup in a toast. "What shall we call the agency?"

"How about Mrs B and Mr H?" He laughed.

"That's no good. I won't be Mrs B for much longer. How about Little Mellington Private Investigation Agency?"

"I think that would be rather wonderful. Yes. I shall talk to a friend of mine about getting cards printed. How exciting." He reached over the table and kissed her gently. "I'm going to look forward to going to work every single day."

"Yes indeed. I shall look forward to it too." Mrs B checked her cup and found that there was a little left. "Very good tea." She nodded to herself.

64.

Mrs B's reunion

Mrs Pendle's kitchen had been in a mess, but an hour and a good deal of hot soapy water had brought up back up to scratch.

"How are you feeling?" Mrs B passed a cup of ginger tea to Mrs Pendle.

"Tired most of the time. A little one, who has discovered the joys of crawling, and the farm, as well as another baby on the way, it's all a bit much." She ran her hand over her stomach, which was rounder than it had been.

"I am sure that it is. Of course, Will and I would be happy to babysit if you wanted a good night's sleep. You know that." Mrs B wiped down the last bit of the table.

"No, good grief, you do enough, and I hear that you two are setting up in business now! I am so pleased for you. The wedding will be coming up soon too. I'm amazed you find time to come down here and sort out my mucky kitchen." She laughed.

"I will always find time for you." Mrs B smiled

and pulled her coat on. "I hope you can have half an hour with your feet up now." She waved from the door and let herself out.

"Mrs B?" Pamela stood in the lane, transferring her weight from one foot to the other.

"Pamela? Good grief, I have been thinking about you this morning. How are you." Mrs B rushed to wrap her arms around the girl.

"I am so sorry. I wanted to tell you the truth about Dad. It would never have worked. It was unfair after you had been so lovely to me." Tears ran from Pamela's eyes.

"No apology required. Come along home with me and have a cup of tea. You can tell me all your news and I can tell you mine." Mrs B linked arms with Pamela and they walked up the hill together.

"I have a favour to ask. I know I have no business asking, and if you say no, I will not be at all surprised." Pamela took a deep breath. "I have to go and visit my mother in prison. She is very angry now that she knows what happened. I wondered if you might come with me. I'm a bit frightened."

"Of course I will come with you. Though I cannot believe that your mother would be worried by my presence. If it gives you some comfort, I would be happy to come along." Mrs B stopped outside her back door. "You know you don't have to visit her, don't you?"

"I do have to. She still has a great many associates outside prison who could make life difficult for me and for Dad." Pamela scowled.

"When will you go?" Mrs B tipped her head on one side.

"This afternoon. If you're free." Pamela smiled.

"Let me check with Will, and see if he can drive us." Mrs B slipped into the kitchen, and returned a moment later, followed by Will, with his car keys in his hand.

"Right – ho ladies. Let's go, shall we?" He opened the car doors and let them into the car. "Good to see you, Pamela."

65.

Mrs B is amazed

The prison building towered above them, dark against the cloudy sky. "Are you sure about this? They will only allow two visitors. I will have to wait outside for you." Will watched their response carefully.

"There will be guards there all the time. We will be perfectly safe." Mrs B smiled up into his face and planted a gentle kiss on his cheek. He watched them walk in and climbed back into the car to wait.

The noise inside was unsettling, gates clanged, and children waiting to go in to see their mothers were fractious. "Thank you for coming with me, Mrs B. I know I am asking a lot."

"Nonsense. I think this might put your mind at rest, to know that your mother has forgiven you." Mrs B had no reason to believe that, other than she was looking for something positive to say.

"You really are a hoot! My mother has never forgiven anyone for anything." Pamela stepped forward in line and held out her arms to be searched by the guard.

When they were sitting at the table, the prisoners were allowed through. Mrs Bisley looked a little less fearsome in her prison uniform, but only a little.

"Pammie? You came. You didn't need to bring her with you." She sat down heavily opposite them.

"I wanted her to come. She has been my friend, and she has looked after me." Pamela pulled herself back from the table. Mrs B was aware of the similarities between them, and the tension in the air, too.

"The police say that you will be giving evidence against me." She took a long, deep breath. "I am surprised by your lack of loyalty. We have always understood that we owe each other a debt of gratitude and we stay loyal to each other in this family, I thought."

"No. That is untrue. You have always demanded my obedience. Dad was always loyal to you, despite your behaviour. That is not the same." Pamela sat up straighter.

"When did I demand anything from you?" Mrs Bisley leaned her elbows on the table.

"You demanded that I marry the dreaded Leonard." Pamela shook her head. "That was the last straw. Dad and I had lived a secret life, hiding everything from you for years, but we couldn't see any way out of the wedding."

"Secret life? What are your talking about?" Mrs Bisley spat the words.

"When I was a child, I used to listen to you telling him before you went out. 'Leave her to cry, no molly-coddling.' We used to wait until your car was gone and then we would play and he would tell me stories. It was the best time. He danced and sang and so did I. We were pirates or dragons or whatever the story called for. He danced and sang and so did I, then we would drink cocoa and eat sweeties, until he would check his watch and say that you would be home soon, and playtime was over. When you sent me away to school, he sent me letters every day. Long stories and silly jokes. I used to write back to him at the gym, under the name of Mr Parker. He said it would stop any nosy parkers reading the letters." Pamela swiped at the tears that spilled. "He made my childhood wonderful. He was the sunshine in my otherwise dreary days."

"You needed to be tough. Life is not easy for women, especially in this family." Mrs Bisley stretched her fingers out towards her daughter.

"Yes. I know it was tough for you when you were growing up. You couldn't wait to leave it behind. But I'm no Annie Bisley. I am not even a Bisley anymore. Granny Bembridge always said you were hard-hearted." Pamela smiled at the effect her words had on her mother. She had meant to wound.

"My name is Annabel. I have not been Annie since I was a child. When did you see my mother?" Mrs Bisley bristled.

"I see my granny every week. She misses you." Pamela's voice caught on the words.

"I had to make choices. My brother died in the war. He was supposed to take over the business from my father. My mother was weak, my sisters were worse than useless." She shook her head. "Do you think this was the life I chose?"

"Yes. Maybe not to start with, but you loved the power it gave you. The business was only part of it." Pamela whispered the words, leaning close to her mother.

"I started out with no power. My father was the one with all the power. He ran the docks before the war, but he never made the money I made. We lived in a rundown house in a tatty part of town." She shook her head. "When we got the telegram about my brother, my father fell apart. I took over the business, running everything in his name. In six months, we were making more money than he had made in a lifetime." She shook her head. "Your grandpa was ill, and he only survived my brother for eight months, it wasn't enough time for me to establish the business. The family wanted to go back to the old ways. I chose to find a different man to hide behind and left them where they were. It's that simple."

"That is not simple. She's not well, and I need your help to get her through it." Pamela's eyes filled with tears.

"I gave clear instructions that you were not to see my mother. When did you meet her?" Mrs Bisley's eyes narrowed.

"Dad always took me, every week." Pamela reached across the table.

"It seems you have inherited my ability to keep secrets." Mrs Bisley smiled for the first time since they had arrived.

"So, you'll help me?" Pamela seemed hopeful. Her mother nodded. It was small, but definitely there.

"Well, I am amazed. I did not expect any of that. The pair of you are so similar, and yet more different than I would have thought possible." Mrs B. jumped when the alarm rang.

"That's visiting time over. Come and see me again and I will do what I can. Thank you for the second chance, Pammie." Mrs Bisley stood and walked away with a stiff back.

"Good heavens. I would like very much to meet your grandmother. You are an inspiring young woman, Pamela. Are you ready to go home?" Mrs B held out her hand.

"I am. To be honest, I think we are both in need of a cup of tea." Pamela took Mrs B's hand in hers and they left the prison together.

66.

Mrs B remembers her trump card

"Mrs B? I need to talk to you, if you have some time?" Pamela gripped the back of one of the kitchen chairs.

"Of course. I need to go and see Mrs Chambers shortly, but I always have time for a cup of tea and a chat." Mrs B poured a cup for Pamela and pushed it across the table.

"Thank you. The thing is, my mother is a difficult person. My granny is a bit difficult too, but in a completely different way. I love my mother, but if she is found guilty of murder, she could hang. It would be my fault if I give evidence against her." Pamela's eyes were red around the edges and tears slipped down her cheeks.

"Yes, I definitely see that your mother is a contrary personality. But if she is guilty of a murder, that is not your fault. I have to see Arnold later today, so I will have a chat with him about it. If I am honest, though, you have given a great deal of evidence to Arnold, which might be enough to convict her without you attending court." Mrs B sipped from her cup.

"My granny is extremely angry. I have never seen her so furious, and trust me, she has been angry almost all of my life." Pamela quirked a smile.

"Why on earth is she angry?" Mrs B reached for Pamela's hand. "I would have thought she would be proud of you."

"My mum's family are, I suppose, what you would call 'salt of the earth.' There are rules." She ticked them off on her fingers. "You look after your own. You keep the family secrets. Family before anything else. No matter what. I've broken every rule. She's on the point of disowning me."

"Is that what happened between your mother and your granny? Did she disown your mother?" Mrs B's brows pushed together.

"No, not at all. My mother walked away from the family. They refused to take orders from her, so she left them behind. That's what she does." Pamela tipped her head to one side. "She tried to help them out, here and there, you know. Paid the bills and helped them with money, but they were shut out of the business and her life."

"What did you know about the assistant manager at the club where I met you?" Mrs B picked up her cup.

"Jamie? He was having a thing with Maureen, but

only for a short time. Most of the time he was in his office I suppose he wasn't around a lot." Pamela reached for her cup.

"He was the assistant manager. Do you know who the manager was?" Mrs B waited while Pamela thought about it.

"I know who the manager is, but if I tell you, I will be breaking one of granny's rules." Pamela trapped her bottom lip between her teeth.

"I know who the manager is too, I just wanted to know if you would tell me the truth. Thank you. I'm grateful, and I know that you will tell me what you can, without putting people you love in danger. It's the best that we can ever do." Mrs B patted Pamela's hand.

"You're not upset?" Pamela's brows pushed together.

"I'm delighted." Mrs B reached across and kissed Pamela on the cheek. "It means I can trust you."

"Auntie? Sorry I didn't realise you had company. Hello Pamela." Arnold took a seat at the table.

"Don't worry on my behalf. I was just going anyway. I've taken up too much time. Thank you, Mrs B. I'll pop in tomorrow, and bring my granny. She'd like to meet you." Pamela waved from the door.

"I need to talk to you, Arnold. I believe that Mr Peters is a very unpleasant man, but not a murderer. Worse than that. I believe that I know exactly who killed Matthew Brunswick."

67.

Mrs B ties the threads together

"Will? We need to get going. I have the last piece of the puzzle. I saw it the other day, but I was slow at putting it together." Mrs B took his hand.

"Fair enough, where's Arnold? I picked up something for you. You can open it in the car while we drive. Where are we going, by the way?"

"To Potterton, my love. Arnold will meet us there. He had to pick something up." She smiled across at him while he drove away from the cottage.

"The parcel there on the seat is for you." He raised his eyebrows and waited for her to untie the string that held the brown paper around the box.

"Oh Will. The cards, you ordered the cards. Little Mellington Investigation Agency. We are official." She beamed. "May I give one to Arnold?"

"I shall remind you if you forget." He laughed.

Will followed her directions and parked the car outside the nightclub. They tried the front door, but it was too early for the club to be open. Mrs B led Will around the side of the building and in through the kitchen. They pushed through the doors and into the bar area.

"I think I know where the person I wish to speak to is likely to be." She led him up the stairs to the staff area. "Mr Grainger?" The man in the staff room turned towards her. "Ah, Mr Grainger, Ben I believe?"

"Yes. Hello. How are you?" He had been pinning up a new staff rota.

"I am fine, thank you. But I am here with bad news." She pulled out a chair for him and sat opposite. Will took another chair at the table. "I worked out how you did it, and I think I know why, too. It took me a little while, but sadly I was distracted, and I missed the truth."

"What are you talking about?" He sat up straighter.

"I found a piece of paper on Jamie Peter's desk when he was arrested. It was in Matthew Brunswick's handwriting. I thought it said 'I think it's big. The stock take is all wrong.' But I was wrong, wasn't I?" He pushed his chair back to find that Will had hold of his wrists.

"Sit down, Mr Grainger." His voice was a growl. The man sank into the chair.

"When Mr Peters showed you the note, you

knew you had to deal with your friend, who had discovered that you had been stealing from the club. It said B.G. Not big. He had caught you. I don't know how, but he knew it was you." Mrs B took a deep breath. "I was wrong. I thought Jamie Peters had found Mr Brunswick beaten by the boys from the boxing club, but it was you. My theory is that they left, and you had found a pair of boxing gloves. Perhaps you got them from the gym or maybe one of them left the gloves behind, but you pushed broken pieces of glass into the gloves and you punched. Your friend died of the injuries you gave him. I gave the paperwork from Mr Peter's desk to the police. My nephew will be here to collect you in a few minutes." Mrs B shook her head. "You knew Matthew for such a long time. It must have been hard to do what you did."

"I'm admitting to nothing." He snarled.

"Well now, that is a shame. Jamie Peters is singing a very different tune, and your name is coming up all over the place." Arnold leaned against the frame of the door.

"Thank you for coming, Arnold." Mrs B smiled up at her nephew.

"Thank you for solving the murder for us, Auntie." He leaned down to kiss her cheek. "I'll take Mr Grainger to the police station."

"Oh, one thing I need to give you, Arnold?" He turned and raised an eyebrow while he slipped the handcuffs onto his captive's wrists.

Mrs B opened her handbag and passed him a small piece of card. "Our card. We are now official."

He scanned the printing. "Congratulations. I'll make sure that the boss knows. I am very proud of you both." He took Mr Grainger away with him.

"I'm very proud of you, too." Will leaned down to put a kiss on her cheek.

"That is the first murder solved by The Little Mellington Investigation Agency. I think we should celebrate. Would you like fish and chips for tea?"

"I think that would be wonderful." He offered her his arm, and she slipped her hand into the crook of his elbow. "I'd think bread and butter to be a wonderful dinner if I was eating it with you."

68.

Mrs B receives a payment

"Oh, my." Mrs B sat down at her kitchen table. The envelope had seemed ordinary enough. "Whatever am I going to do about this?" Marmalade walked carefully through the kitchen. Going to his bowl, and finding it empty, he mewed loudly. "Sorry Marmalade. I should have given you breakfast." Mrs B put some food into Marmalade's bowl. "There you are."

"Hello?" Will knocked on the back door. "Are you at home?"

"I am." Mrs B watched him walk in and come to join her at the table.

"Good morning, my love." He kissed her on the cheek.

"Better than good. Take a look at what came through the post today." She pushed the envelope across the table.

He raised an eyebrow and opened the envelope. "Oh well, there we go. Our first payment as a detective agency. This is quite unbelievable. I think this is about half my yearly salary when I was a chief inspector. Good grief." He opened the letter and scanned the closely cramped writing. "Mr Bisley? He paid us for the investigation that proved his innocence? Well, what a way to start."

"If it carries on like this, we will have no problem paying the bills." Mrs B laughed.

"I saw Arnold this morning, and he told me that he has told the new Chief Inspector about our new business and that they will be charged for any further help." He laughed. "We seem to be off and running."

"Would you have time to take this cheque to the bank?" Mrs B watched him think about it. "I wanted to call in on Mrs Pendle today, and check how she is."

"Of course. Come with me to the bank first. I will need you to sign some papers. The bank account for the agency will be in both our names. Equal partners means equal in everything." He reached for her hands.

"Partners." She squeezed his hands.

They drove to the bank and Mrs B signed the forms next to his signature. The manager shook her hand and wished them both good luck with the business.

"I'll drop you to Mrs Pendle and see you later for dinner. I might even make dinner, if we have something not too complicated." He laughed and pulled up outside the Pendle farm. He leaned across and kissed her tenderly. "I love that we have dinner together every day. Soon, perhaps I won't have to go home every night." He raised an eyebrow and laughed.

"I like our dinners too. We will be living together soon, imagine that? I will wake up in the morning, and there you will be." She smiled across at him.

"I imagine very little else, my love." He pulled her close for a kiss and let her go slowly and regretfully.

"Mrs Pendle? Hello. How are you feeling today?" Mrs B picked up the little boy who was crawling across the kitchen. "How are you? Are you hungry?" She opened the cupboard and pulled out a bowl, balancing the toddler on her hip. Once he was installed in the high chair, Mrs B spooned the pureed fruit into his mouth. When he had finished the bowl, she gave him a cup of milk and rocked him to sleep. Wherever his mother was, she would not leave him alone without a very good reason. "Sleep well, little one." She kissed his head and popped him into his cot. "I have to find your mother."

69.

Mrs B finds Mrs Pendle

"Hello? Hello? Are you here?" Mrs B walked through the house and out into the farmyard, calling as she went. Mr Pendle drove into the yard on a tractor and stopped by the barn. "Mr Pendle, I am so pleased to see you. Do you know where your wife is?"

"She should be here. I have only been gone an hour. I had to check on the top field. Is little Jack alright?" He jumped from the seat of the tractor.

"I have fed your son and put him to bed. Please, will you help me find Mrs Pendle?" A noise from one of the pig pens had them both running. "Mrs Pendle? Are you there?"

"Mrs B? Oh, am I glad to see you. I was cleaning out the pigs, Grizelda's such a messy girl, and I felt dizzy. The thing is, I don't seem to be able to stand up." Tears ran down her face. She was frightened.

"Well then, let's get you up and back to the house. A good meal and a hot cup of tea will help." Mrs B pushed herself under Mrs Pendle's arm and waited for Mr Pendle to help. He shook his head and scooped his wife off her feet. "Good idea, Mr Pendle."

In the house, Mrs B pulled off Mrs Pendle's boots and helped her out of her coat. "I feel a little better. Perhaps I was just tired. Thank you for looking after Jack."

"I think a good night's sleep might be an idea. Do you need me to help you upstairs?" Mrs B held Mrs Pendle's hands. "Perhaps have the doctor take a look, just to be sure in the morning?"

"I'll get her upstairs. Thank you, Mrs B." Mr Pendle carried his wife up the stairs.

"I will pop in first thing in the morning to make sure everything is alright. Sleep well." Mrs B let herself out of the door and walked home with a heavy heart.

70.

Mrs B asks for a favour

"Pamela? Good morning, dear. Could you ask your husband if he would please pop in to see Mrs Pendle. She collapsed yesterday, and I am worried." Mrs B's brows pushed together.

"Of course. I'll pop and ask him now. Then I have someone I want you to meet." She walked through and knocked on the doctor's office. "All sorted. He's going down there now. Come and have a cup of tea. I have a visitor."

Mrs B followed Pamela through to the kitchen and found an older lady sitting at the table. "Mrs Bembridge, I believe."

"My granddaughter told me you were good, but I didn't believe her. More fool me, I suppose. I think you know my daughter and my son-in-law. He's a good man. I need to apologise for my daughter though. She's a hard one. She was a lovely girl when she was a kiddie. Gentle and kind. Hard to believe now, I suppose." Mrs Bembridge pulled a crumpled handkerchief out of her sleeve and wiped her nose.

"No child is bad, Mrs Bembridge. They are all rather lovely. They're clean and fresh when they come to us, aren't they?" Mrs B took a seat opposite Mrs Bembridge and accepted the cup of tea that Pamela offered. "Thank you, Pamela."

"She wasn't bad, you're right. She changed when my son died. I think she felt she had to, but she didn't. Perhaps I relied on her a little too much, but losing my boy like that, it broke me." Mrs Bembridge wiped her eyes. "I want to make my peace with her. I don't have too long, and I don't want to leave this life without sorting it out with my girl. Pammie has been the joy of my life, but I need to sort it out with my Annie." She reached back to hold Pamela's hand, which rested on her shoulder.

"Can I do anything to help?" Mrs B sipped from her cup.

"Actually, yes, I think you can. It's a lot to ask, but I need to talk to my daughter without Pammie there and I'm not strong enough to go alone. Would you come with me?" Mrs Bembridge raised her eyebrows.

"If you think it will help, of course I will. I shall ask Will if he would be able to take us. Let me know when you want to go." Mrs B nodded to herself.

"Mrs B?" Pamela's husband came into the kitchen, his medical bag in his hand. "I have to thank you for today." He held out his hand. "Mrs Pendle is on the way to the hospital. She is unwell, and she could have lost the baby, or worse. Your instincts are good."

"Heavens! Will Mrs Pendle be alright? Who is looking after little Jack? Mr Pendle will be busy with the farm." Mrs B jumped to her feet.

"Mrs Pendle will be in the very best place. She is still in danger, but I am confident that we reached her in time. I think Mr Pendle would be grateful for your help if you have time." He smiled and watched her gather her coat and bag.

"I am sorry, Pamela, but I should go. Mrs Bembridge, I am happy to have met you. Perhaps let me know when you would like me to accompany you?" Mrs B waited for a nod from both of them and pulled on her coat, letting herself out into the blustery day outside.

71.

Mrs B and Mrs Bembridge

Will parked the car carefully outside the prison and helped Mrs Bembridge to the door. "Please be careful. Both of you."

"Thank you, Will." Mrs B squeezed his arm. "See you in a little while."

Wheezing and struggling to catch her breath, Mrs Bembridge gripped the table and gratefully accepted the cup of water that Mrs B fetched for her. "Thank you. Pammie said you were kind. I'm always suspicious of kind, I wonder what people are after. But you helped her, and now you're helping me. Sorry if I was a bit prickly."

"No reason why you should trust me. Sometimes you need to know someone a little while before you build trust. Ah, here she is." Mrs B watched Mrs Bisley walk to the table.

"Oh good, just what I hoped for." Mrs Bisley shook her head.

"Pammie said you agreed to talk to me. Before we start, I wanted to thank you for agreeing. We have had our differences, but we both love that girl. She's a credit to you and her father." Mrs Bembridge's shoulders heaved as she shook with a fresh bout of coughing.

"She said that you aren't well. What's wrong with you?" Mrs Bisley leaned towards her mother. The blunt question and the tone were a shock to Mrs B, but she tried her best to hide it.

"Straight to the point. My lungs are finished. They don't work anymore. I've a few weeks, maybe even a couple of months, then I'll be gone. Nobody will be left who will remember when you were a little one. Or that you hated eating cabbage." Mrs Bembridge was coughing again.

"I quite like cabbage now. I think it was the way you cooked it." Mrs Bisley gave half a smile.

"You always were a cheeky little mare. May God forgive me, although I had six children, you were always my favourite. Your brother, he was a little so and so, but he was my only boy. I believed he would carry on the business with your dad. When we had the telegram to say your brother was gone, and then only three months later I lost your sisters to the pleurisy, I was broken. I had nothing left to give. It was wrong of me. I should have been stronger. I'm sorry Annie." She reached halfway across the table.

"You should have been. Dad should have too. Since I was a child, I despised weakness. I tried to make Pammie strong, but he crossed me at every turn, and you helped him. Behind my back. I paid your way for years, covered your rent, and your bills. You could have lived in a better house, had an easier life, but you held your disapproval for me closer to your heart than the love you should have given your daughter. It didn't stop you taking my money though, did it?" Mrs Bisley shook her head. "Now you come to tell me that you loved me all the time. As though that will heal the wound that hangs between us. You are not long for this world." She reached across the other half of the table to hold her mother's hands. "Neither am I. My lungs are strong, but whether I am found guilty and face the hangman or the disease that is eating me from the inside sees me off first is the only question. I have not told Pammie. It is not fair to worry her. I would be grateful if you would keep my illness secret."

"Oh Annie, are you in pain?" Mrs Bembridge wrapped her hands around her daughter's fingers.

"I am. But it is not so bad. What is Pammie to do, without me or you?" Mrs Bisley's eyes swam with tears. "She has nobody else."

"Her father will be there for her, and he will help her." Mrs Bembridge nodded. "They have always had a special bond. Both of them laugh at the same things."

"I will tell you, because you know how the

business works, to an extent. The men who once worked for me have been well paid for years. Now that I am no longer able to control things, I have set them up to run things. They will be a consortium of sorts. Of course, it will not be long until they are all at each other's throats, but it will mean they fight each other rather than going after my girl or her father."

"I will keep your secret. But perhaps if Pammie knew how brave you have been, it might heal some troubles between you." Mrs Bembridge tipped her head to one side.

"No. She will need none of that. I have made sure she will be safe. I do not need her gratitude. Or yours. The truth is, I have never needed anyone. I have always been quite enough on my own." Mrs Bisley turned away from her mother to face Mrs B. "Can I count on your silence?"

"I will promise you that." Mrs B nodded. "I have misjudged you. If I am honest, I believed you to be cold-blooded, but your love and courage for your daughter has proved me wrong. I owe you an apology."

"Fair enough." Mrs Bisley stood and leaned heavily on the table. "Good of you to come and see me."

Mrs B watched Mrs Bisley walk away and found that there were tears on her cheeks.

"I always said it would bring bad luck." Mrs

Bembridge shook her head. "A change of the name, but not of the letter, is a change for the worse, and not for the better. People say these things are old wives' tales, or superstition, but they are wisdom handed down from the generations before. She should never have married Bisley. He's a good man, but he was the wrong one for her. She needed someone stronger." She shook her head. "Thank you for coming with me today. Promise you'll keep an eye on our Pammie? With both of us gone, she will need you and her father."

"Indeed, I will, Mrs Bembridge, I absolutely will." Mrs B helped Mrs Bembridge to her feet and began the walk back to the car where Will was waiting. She smiled at the thought. She would be changing her name soon, and the first letter too. Very soon she would be Mrs H. Perhaps Mrs Bembridge would approve.

72.

Mrs B visits the hospital

"I will wait here while you visit. I think she would be more comfortable talking to you if I am not there." Will pulled out a newspaper and sat down to read it. "Take your time, no rush."

Mrs B nodded and pushed through the double doors into the ward. Mrs Pendle was sitting up in bed, looking a good deal better than the last time Mrs B had seen her.

"Mrs Pendle, how are you feeling?" Mrs B reached for her friend's hand.

"Mrs B! I am so pleased to see you. I am feeling fine, but they will not let me out of bed. They say that the baby would be at risk. My blood pressure is too high, they say. It's ridiculous. I am needed back on the farm." She shook her head at the silliness.

"Quite the reverse. Mr Pendle is managing the farm and Mrs Chambers and Mrs Appleby are taking turns caring for your little Jack. They are all working hard so that you can rest and keep his baby brother or sister safe. You are a wonderful mother, and you can be again, this time around, by staying here and allowing others to take care of you." Mrs B reached across and took Mrs Pendle's hands in her own. "Now I have a great deal to tell you. The doctor says that you will be able to come home in the next few weeks, and we will all be helping until then. Your little lad has the whole village to take care of him. And while they care for him, they care for you."

"Why on earth would everyone be so kind? They all have busy lives. It is above and beyond." Mrs Pendle began to cry a little.

"They are kind. You're right. But it's because you have helped us all over the years. You're a very wonderful friend, and we all love you dearly." Mrs B patted her hand. "In any case, I need you to be better in time for my wedding. Mrs Lennet and Barbara have planned all sorts of surprises, and it would not be any kind of wedding at all unless you were there."

Outside, Will waited. He was pleased to see Mrs B. "How was she?"

"Distressed. But I believe she will agree to stay here until she is better, which is a good step forward." She smiled and took his hand.

"Well, that is good news, because I believe I have found our next case." He folded the newspaper and passed it to her.

"Oh my, yes indeed." She nodded. "We will need

to start right away. I suggest we speak to Arnold and find out what the police are doing about it."

"My thoughts exactly." Will offered his arm, and they made their way out of the hospital.

73.

Mrs B and the new adventure

"Arnold, have you looked at this story?" Mrs B was becoming increasingly anxious.

"I have, and I understand what you're saying, but I don't get to choose which cases we investigate. That is much higher up the chain of command, as well you know." Arnold shook his head.

"Fine, can you tell me if the family have contacted you?" Mrs B held onto Arnold's arm.

"Yes, they had plenty to say, but there is nothing that I can do without permission. The higher ups will tell me when they decide to investigate." He shrugged.

"Right, we had better contact the family. See you later Arnold." Mrs B and Will left the police station.

"Should we go to the family? We could drop a note in through the door, offer our help, I suppose, or should we visit?" Will kept pace with Mrs B up the hill.

"I think we might find that we need to do

neither." Mrs B pointed to her back door as they came level. "Good afternoon. May we help?"

"Thank goodness. I've been trying to find you. I have been recommended by my friend, Mrs Lennet. She told me that you are very helpful. Please help me find my husband. I went to the police, but they said that he is an adult and is allowed to leave me if he wishes." Tears spilled from the lady's eyes.

"Oh, my dear, come inside. Let's sit down and find out a little more." Mrs B ushered the lady inside.

"I should have introduced myself. I do apologise, I am Mrs Endersleigh. My husband, Norman, he is a fussy man. Every day for years he walked around checking for dust on the furniture and tutting at everything. He was a difficult person to live with, but I have always loved him. He might have complained and moaned about things, but he loved me, too. I know that he did." She wiped her eyes and took a breath.

Mrs B sat across the table from her, and Will joined them. "What changed?"

"Something happened about a week ago. I really cannot tell you what. I went to lunch with Mrs Lennet, and when I came back, he was completely strange. He said he had received a message from his mother, and he needed to know more. The woman passed away five years ago. He was quite excitable. That in itself was strange." She shook her head.

"Was he interested in the occult or any such thing?" Will watched her carefully.

"No. It was entirely out of the blue. Now he is gone, and I am at a loss to imagine what sort of danger he might be in." Her voice shook. "I cannot imagine that he would do that of his own choice. He is just not that sort of person."

"Did he tell you how the message arrived?" Mrs B watched her carefully.

"Oh yes, that was the strange part. A woman knocked at the door. While I was out at lunch." She shook her head at the absurdity of the idea.

"Do you know who she was?" Will watched carefully.

"Oh yes. I know all about her, but nobody will listen. The only people investigating it is the local paper." Mrs Endersleigh opened her handbag and pulled out a small business card. She pushed it over the table.

"Well now. That looks like a lead we should be following up. I shall make you a cup of tea, and then we will be on our way to speak with…" She lifted the card to read it. "Mrs Eileen Faversham."

"A cup of tea. Yes, that's a good idea. You will take the case, then?" Mrs Endersleigh seemed much happier than she had been.

"Yes indeed. We would be glad to." Will smiled while Mrs B put the kettle on.

74.

Mrs B meets Mrs Faversham

"Here we are. This is the address on the card. It looks very normal. I expected some sort of spooky place. Is that strange of me?" Mrs B turned to Will, her eyebrow raised.

"No, I wasn't sure what to expect, either." They stood together at the gate.

"We had better go and see if we can find the lady." Mrs B shrugged and took the three steps it took to travel from the gate to the door. She raised the knocker and tapped.

"Hello?" The woman was younger than Mrs B, sharp featured and pinched around the eyes.

"Mrs Faversham? Good afternoon. I wonder if you might spare us a few minutes?" Mrs B tipped her head to one side and smiled.

"With regard to?" The skin around Mrs Faversham's mouth tightened.

"I believe that you receive messages from those who have passed on." Mrs B smiled as hopefully as she could.

"Yes. Sometimes I do. I have no message for you." Mrs Faversham lifted her chin.

"You had a message for a friend of mine, a Mr Endersleigh. I wondered if you might share the message with me?" Mrs B smiled her friendliest smile.

"Messages are only intended for the person they are for. Not for anyone else." Mrs Faversham crossed her arms around her body.

"Yes, true, I appreciate that. However, the police are now interested in Mr Endersleigh, and will want to talk to people who have spoken to him in the last few weeks. That would include you. I know that you would rather avoid the upheaval of that sort of visit. If you could let me have the message, I will try my best to have the police tick you off their list without a visit." Mrs B rested her hand against the brickwork around the door.

Mrs Faversham pushed the door a little closer to being closed. "I told him his mother wanted him to know that he was loved and that his father was in danger."

"Where did you get the message from?" Mrs B's brows pushed together.

"I hear the messages. Not always the same way. Usually when I'm relaxed." She shrugged.

"Thank you. May I come back and visit you?" Mrs B waited for her response.

"I'd really rather that you didn't. If it's all the same to you." Mrs Faversham pushed the door closed, leaving them standing on the pathway.

"Well, I suppose we need to find out who Mr Endersleigh's father is." Will opened the gate and waited for Mrs B to walk through. "You really shouldn't say that you could stop the police visiting." He shook his head. "It isn't true."

"Of course it's true. I can ask Arnold not to visit. That's the same thing." She smiled up at him. "I know it was a little deceitful, but I could see there were things she wanted to hide. She kept pushing the door shut, and I thought it might encourage her to tell me."

"I love you, but yes, it was deceitful, and yes, it worked." He kissed her gently. "Clever thing."

75.

Mrs B goes looking

The bus ride from Little Mellington to Potterton was one of Mrs B's greatest pleasures. While she enjoyed travelling in Will's car, and the good chance it gave them to chat, the peace of sitting on a bus on her own and giving herself the chance to think things through had often given her the answers she was looking for.

It was a pleasant enough morning, even if the wind was blowing the clouds around, and she watched the fields out of the window, with her handbag held firmly on her knee. Will had gone to the dentist and would not be available until lunchtime. He had arranged to collect her near the bus station in Potterton, and that suited her just fine.

Her first stop was to visit Mr McKinley, who she hoped would be at home. As it happened, he was outside, unloading some boxes from a van. "Good morning, Mr McKinley. Are you well?"

"Mrs B. I am. Do you have time for a cup of tea? I was about to make some." Mr Mckinley smiled widely and led her inside. He filled the kettle from the tap and lit the gas on the stove to heat it. "Nice as it is to see you, I imagine that you have not come here just for tea." He turned and smiled as she lifted a package out onto the table.

"You're right. I am grateful for the tea, though, and I brought some biscuits I baked yesterday for you. I need to know about Mrs Eileen Faversham Can you help?" Mrs B unwrapped the package and waited while Mr McKinley thought about the question.

"I know of her. She set herself up as a fortune teller sort of thing. I think most of the girls like to be told they'll meet a handsome stranger and live happily ever after. It's not always like that in life, but there's no harm in it." He poured the water into the teapot as he spoke and put out cups and saucers, along with a small jug of milk. "That was all it was until a few months ago. She told one of the lads who works for me that he was going to be arrested. I looked into it and found out that he had paid her a fair amount to make sure it didn't happen. I have heard that she has charged a lot of people a great deal of money for information or protection against some bad luck. I don't believe in that sort of thing, but people do, I suppose." He shrugged and poured the tea.

"Does she work with anyone else do you know?" Mrs B accepted the cup that he passed her.

"I don't know, but I do think that she has branched out from her old way of doing things." He helped himself to a biscuit. "Sometimes people just come up with a new idea, a way to make a bit more money, I suppose."

"What about Mr and Mrs Endersleigh? Do you know them?" Mrs B sipped her tea.

"He's the bank manager. Nice enough. I did hear that some money went missing, but he always maintained that it was an accounting error, and the bank kept him on, so it can't have been anything that was provable." Mr McKinley laughed. "They don't steal like proper thieves, they're smarter than that. Too respectable to get their hands dirty."

"Have you heard from Tommy and Maisie lately? I imagine that you will be excited about being a grandfather soon." She sipped from her cup.

"I am. They're up in Birmingham this week. Tommy's trying to get Maisie to take it a little easier, but you know what she's like. She does three shows a day sometimes." He looked thoughtful for a while. "I've not really thanked you properly for being a friend to my Tommy, have I?"

"You have been a friend to me, Mr McKinley, and that is thanks enough. Your son is a wonderful young man, and I am proud to call him my friend." She smiled and nodded before pushing the package of biscuits towards him. "Enjoy the biscuits." She left him at the kitchen table.

The bank was in the middle of the High Street, it was one of three different banks which had branches in Potterton. She had never set foot in the building before, and stood outside for a minute to get her courage together.

"Good morning, Madam." The young man greeted her when she reached the front of the queue.

"Good morning. I am looking for a little advice. My husband and I have some savings and we would like to open an account which would pay us some interest. I wonder if I could speak to the manager about it?" She smiled her most innocent smile and waited.

"Most small savings account can be dealt with here on the front desk." He nodded and tried to look professional.

"Yes, but this is money from the sale of one of our houses. I need to be certain that it will be safe." She smiled again and watched the young man's eyebrows lift towards his hairline.

"Certainly. Would you take a seat and I will see if the assistant manager is available." He left his seat and almost ran to the

A short, wide gentleman rushed out of the office and came to stand in front of Mrs B. "Good morning, madam. How fortuitous that you chose to call in this morning. I am free for the next half an hour. Mr Pilston at your service.

"Thank you, Mr Pilston. I am Mrs Hunton. I am so glad that you can see me. I shall be meeting my husband for lunch and I will be able to tell him that I have done some research on where to place our savings." Mrs B took his offered hand, glad that she was, as always, wearing gloves, which would stop him from spotting the lack of a wedding ring on her finger, and allowed him to show her into the manager's office.

76.

Mrs B finds out more than she expected

"Here we are. Now, I understand that you have some savings that you wish to deposit." Mr Pilston gripped his hands together and leaned them on the leather-topped desk.

"We will do, once the sale of one of our houses goes through. I want to make sure that the money will earn some interest while it is on deposit with you." Mrs B sat back into the thickly upholstered chair. "Do you know, I have been here before. I was not certain. It was a few years ago. I think perhaps you were not the manager then. I spoke to a Mr Enders or a similar name. He was most helpful. I imagine that was your predecessor."

"I am, in fact the assistant manager, Mr Endersleigh is the manager. Although he is not in the branch today." Mr Pilston passed some paperwork over to Mrs B. "These are some of our savings accounts. As you will see, they all offer good rates of interest. You will see a return on your investment." He ran his finger down the list to demonstrate.

"Wonderful. May I take this with me?" Mrs B read through the information. "What a shame Mrs Endersleigh is not here. I do so enjoy renewing an acquaintance. However, presumably he will be back in the branch by the time the sale goes through and I can say hello to him then.

"I very much hope that is the case. Was there anything else that I could help you with?" Mr Pilston waited, fingers interlaced on the desk.

"I am concerned that the money that I deposit with you should be safe. You hear such dreadful things about banks these days. I know my friend refused to step foot inside a bank for fear of losing her money." Mrs B shook her head.

"Any rumours you may have heard about this bank are nothing but groundless gossip, Mrs Hunton." He paused and took a breath. "It was an accounting error, which was put right immediately. No money went missing at all."

"Well, that is good to know. I shall be able to tell my husband that we would be in good hands. It must have been a dreadful worry when it happened, though." Mrs B shook her head sadly.

"Well naturally. We were most concerned, however. Luckily Mr Endersleigh and I stayed here through the night, so determined were we to clear the bank's reputation. I am sorry to say that in the early hours, I closed my eyes for a few minutes. Mr Endersleigh must be made of sterner stuff than I. He continued on, and discovered the error. I can tell you that when he woke me with the news, I was heartily overjoyed. He sent me home to rest and carried on, to put the whole sad matter right." Mr Pilston smiled widely at the memory.

"That is truly wonderful. Are you and Mr Endersleigh both from around here? You may have known my husband as children growing up?" She leaned forward and waiting for an answer.

"No, I was born in Bridlington, quite some distance away. Mr Endersleigh grew up locally. I believe his father still lives in the Potterton area, out of town now though, near to Chesterton." He nodded at Mrs B, entirely certain that he was only passing the time of day with a potential customer.

"Well, that is good to know. I am glad to have met you today, Mr Pilston. I shall bring my husband in to meet you once we are ready to invest." Mrs B stood up and hung her handbag from the crook of her elbow. "If you will excuse me, I still have shopping to do before I meet up with him, and he does dislike me to be late."

"Of course, Mrs Hunton. I look forward to meeting Mr Hunton. Thank you for dropping in today." He opened the office door and shepherded her to the front door. "Good day."

Mrs B smiled to herself. She had the information that she had come for. Her watch said it was a quarter to eleven and Will would be another two hours. She would have time to visit Barbara and see little Jennifer before she met up with him. She might also be able to borrow Barbara's telephone directory.

77.

Mrs B receives a message

"Will? Hello, how did it go with the dentist?" Mrs B opened the car door and slid into the passenger seat.

"Hello. I'm sorry, I didn't see you coming. You must have crept up on me." He laughed and touched his hand to his face.

"Sore?" She smiled.

"A little." He nodded.

"Are you well enough to drive me a little way? I learned a little about Mr Endersleigh while you were busy with your teeth." Mrs B opened her handbag and took out an address.

"You're amazing." He took the paper and read it. "Yes, I know where that is."

When he had parked the car, they walked to the front door together and Mrs B knocked on the door of the bungalow.

A man who looked to be a little over eighty stood in the doorway.

"Good afternoon, Mr Endersleigh. I wonder if

you might be able to help me?" Mrs B smiled and waited hopefully.

"Who are you?" He peered a little closer.

"I am Mrs B. This is Mr Hunton. We are looking for your son." She tipped her head to one side. "He came to see you, didn't he?"

"He did, first time in a long while. I only see him when he's in trouble." He wheezed out a laugh.

"Do you know where he is now? It's urgent that we speak to him. I believe that he may be in some danger, and we are here to protect him. I am certain that you want him to be safe." She nodded, and he nodded with her.

"Yes. You had better come in then." He turned away from them and shuffled his way to the living room, leaving the door open for them to follow him. The exertion left him breathless and pale. "He turned up here three days ago. Said he was in trouble, took some of the things he'd left here a while ago, and left. That's all I know."

"Did you see what he took with him?" Will spoke for the first time.

"Yes. Boxes. From the loft. I can't get up there anymore. It's all his up there." Mr Endersleigh made another wheezing laugh.

"Did he have a car with him?" Will sat back into the sofa.

"Yes, I heard him drive away." Mr Endersleigh

rested his head back and his eyes began to close.

"Thank you, Mr Endersleigh." Mrs B reached across and patted the old man's hand. "We will show ourselves out."

Outside on the road, they climbed back into the car and Will turned to look at Mrs B. "Back to square one, I think."

"Oh no, not at all, my love." We will wait for a little while, and be uncomfortable, but we will be together." She raised an eyebrow and leaned back against the car seat. The daylight faded around them and the evening drew in. "There we are. We have the proof that we need." She pointed to the small skylight in the roof. "Someone is in the loft and has just put the lights on."

Mrs B knocked on the door again and waited for Mr Endersleigh to shuffle his way to open it. "I am so sorry to bother you again, Mr EndIersleigh. I wondered if I might take a look in your loft. It seems your son left the light on when he was last here. You'll be running up the electricity bill for no good reason otherwise."

"Oh, thank you. How kind." He stood back to let her through, and she waited while Will pulled down the loft hatch in the middle of the hallway. It moved smoothly and quietly with a ladder attached, and Will put his foot on the ladder. "Oh no, Will. We don't need to go up. Mr Edersleigh will come down to us, won't you?"

A man's face appeared over the side of the loft hatch. "Hello?"

"I'm a friend of your wife's, Mr Endersleigh. She is very worried about you, but she really doesn't know what has been going on, does she?" Mrs B shook her head and waited for him to decide to climb down the ladder.

"Mr Endersleigh, perhaps it would be wise to explain. If we can find you, then whoever you are hiding from cannot be far behind.

"I will tell you all about it." And he did.

"You had better stay with Will for a few days and bring your dad with you. If things are as bad as you say." Mrs B patted her hands on her knees, and together they trouped out into Will's car. "Where is your car, Mr Edersleigh?"

"I parked it a few streets away." He seemed relieved that someone was taking charge.

"Right then. Let's get you away from here, and safe." Mrs B gently helped the older Mr Endersleigh into the car and they were on their way.

Mrs B poured the milk into her cup of tea. This was and always had been one of her favourite times of the day. A cup of tea in the morning, before everything began. It was a good time to roll thoughts and ideas around in her head.

Mrs Bembridge and Mrs Bisley had been on her

mind since she left the prison. Both of them so unwell and yet focused only on Pamela's welfare. They had more in common than first appearances had suggested. She took a sip from her cup. Both of them had done so much to protect Pamela, just in different ways.

When a knock sounded on the back door, she expected to find Will and the two Endersleighs on the step, but she found Mrs Faversham instead.

"Well, Mrs Faversham, what a surprise." Mrs B waited for the woman to speak.

"I have a message for you, from Herbert." She smiled, confident of the effect of her words, when Mrs B's hand flew to her throat.

"In that case, you had better come in." Mrs B opened the door and moved the small potted geranium from the left side of her step to the right. "That plant will be getting no sun at all where it was. Now, Mrs Faversham, would you like a cup of tea? There's one in the pot."

78.

Mrs B and Mrs Faversham

"Now then, drink your tea and do tell me what has you rushing to my door at this time of the morning." Mrs B pushed a cup of tea across the table.

"I told you. There is a message from Herbert. I suspect that you're interested to hear what he has to say about your upcoming marriage?" Mrs Faversham raised an eyebrow.

"Good heavens, Mrs Faversham. I am quite surprised by what you say. I have never imagined such a thing. To be honest, I am not certain that I want to hear it." She took a sip from her tea. "It goes against the teachings of the church and I will tell you the truth, that I am uncomfortable with the idea. I mean no disrespect to you. This is in no way about you."

"I only pass on the messages. No different from the post office, I suppose. But if you don't want to hear it, I've had a wasted journey. I suppose." She shrugged. "If you don't mind helping me out with the bus fare home? I'm a little short."

"But Mr Endersleigh must have paid you for your message?" Mrs B stood up and went to her coat. She pulled a few coins from her pocket. "This is all I have, I'm afraid."

"Thanks." Mrs Faversham turned back at the door. "I've never had anyone turn down a message before. You're an odd one, Mrs B."

"I may well be, but I cannot be anything other than I am." Mrs B reached out her hand and took Mrs Faversham's hand in hers. "Thank you so much for coming over."

"You are a surprising woman, Mrs B. Can I ask, did you not like Herbert?" Mrs Faversham kept her hand in Mrs B's.

"I loved him. He was a wonderful and kind man." Mrs B smiled. "Far better than I deserved. If you can speak to him. Please send him my love."

Mrs B watched Mrs Faversham walk away down towards the bus stop. There was a great deal of work to do on this case. Mrs B slid the geranium pot back to its original position. There was no need to warn Will to delay his arrival now that her visitor was gone.

79.

Mrs B and Will look more closely

"Morning my love, sorry we're a little later than planned, but it took a while to be ready to leave, with three of us waiting to get in the bathroom." He kissed her cheek tenderly.

"He is being very polite. I am afraid I am slow in the mornings these days." Mr Endersleigh accepted the offer of a chair gratefully.

"Come along and sit down, all of you. The tea will be ready shortly and we really need to find out a little more about what has been going on." Mrs B fetched cups and a plate of biscuits. "Now then. Mr Endersleigh junior, please can you tell us what you have been up to? Because, after all, that is what started all this mess, is it not?"

"Yes, I am sad to say it is all my own fault." Mr Endersleigh held his head in his hands.

"No, I will not allow you to take the blame. I was a bank manager too, and it was me who came up with the idea. For years, I used my scheme to supplement my income, and nobody was ever the wiser. I told my son, and he used my system, but he wanted more, and more quickly. We had to put it back and convince the bank it was an accounting error. To be honest, it was the most fun I'd had in ages." The senior Mr Endersleigh chuckled to himself and accepted a biscuit.

"It was such a simple idea, and it worked beautifully. Most people have no understanding of how interest rates work. They put their wages into the bank each week and just leave it there, earning nothing at all. All we did was place little bits of lots of people's money into accounts which earn interest. We collected the interest and gave them back the money that we had borrowed from them." Mr Endersleigh grinned across the table at his father. "Something of a family business, I suppose."

"Well, I am surprised." Mrs B's eyebrows lifted towards her hairline. "So, how did it all go wrong? How did Mrs Faversham find out?"

"Ah yes. When the bank noticed a small account error my son made, there was an investigation, but they found nothing more than he had made a mistake with the books which was corrected. Mrs Faversham's brother worked for the bank for a little while. A very little while, and gathered that something had gone on. There was gossip, as always. I suspect that she added up all the pieces of the jigsaw and worked out enough to blackmail us." Mr Endersleigh smiled and accepted the cup of tea Mrs B put in front of him.

"Strangely, I had a visit from her this morning." Mrs B sat down at the table. Will's eyebrows shot up. "But what did she ask you for, Mr Endersleigh?"

"Money. A good deal of it. I am sorry to say that I refused. She then threatened that my father would be in danger, and so would I. So, I went to stay to keep him safe, and tried to make myself invisible at the same time. Unfortunately, I failed at both!" Mr Endersleigh reached across and held his father's hand. "Sorry, Dad."

"Hush now. You may be rushing ahead of yourself." Mrs B sipped her tea. "I may just have an idea. Perhaps a little more than that. At present, you are both safe and sound. Are you happy for me to proceed with my plan?"

The two Endersleighs nodded as though their heads had become loose.

80.

Mrs B bites back

In the small café in Potterton, Mrs B poured herself a cup of tea, and smiled when the waitress brought her a toasted teacake. "Thank you, dear."

"Sorry we were out of iced buns. They go so quickly." The young girl smiled.

"Not to worry. A teacake comes a close second." She took a bite and smiled.

"Mrs B?" Mrs Faversham stood at the table. "I received your note."

"Mrs Faversham? What a nice surprise. Would you like a cup of tea?" Mrs B tapped the pot.

"Do you ever do anything except drink tea?" Mrs Faversham slipped into the seat opposite Mrs B.

"Oh yes. I do enjoy a cup, though." Mrs B smiled. "I am so pleased that you came to meet me. I have heard so many conflicting stories about you, and they cannot possibly all be true. Perhaps you might help me with that?"

"If you listen to gossip, Mrs B, I cannot help you."

Mrs Faversham tried her best to look superior.

"No indeed. However, I have heard that your brother has a long and illustrious criminal record. When I visited your home to speak to you, there were things in your hallway which you were worried about me seeing, and they frightened you when I suggested a visit from the police. I think those items were stolen, and your brother had put you under pressure to keep them at your home." Mrs B signalled to the waitress to bring another cup, and poured Mrs Faversham a cup of tea.

"You have no proof of that." Mrs Faversham's superior expression had been replaced by one of concern.

"Do I, or do I not? We may find out later, perhaps?" She sipped her tea.

"My brother had some problems, I'll admit that. But those are far behind him now." Mrs Faversham sipped her tea.

"I am so pleased to hear it. How far behind? Far enough to be out of your house now?" Mrs B shook her head. "Come now, Mrs Faversham. Let us at least tell the truth to each other. Nobody else is here."

"Mrs B. You are right about my brother. But he has changed his ways." Mrs Faversham drank her tea.

"I am very glad to hear it. The truth is, I want very much to believe you." Mrs B reached out to Mrs Faversham and took her hand. "I believe in second chances, too."

"You understand? I am so very pleased." Mrs Faversham appeared to be close to tears.

"Of course. You just want the best for your brother. That is entirely natural. I have been thinking about these messages that you receive. Is that a gift that you have had since childhood?"

"Yes, I have always heard things, but it seems stronger recently. I am not really sure how it works. I simply sit down quietly in my living room and close my eyes, always at nine thirty each evening, and the messages come through." She shrugged.

"That is very exact. My goodness you are more organised than the post office." Mrs B shook her head.

"I suppose it is just the way that it works for me. I am not sure how it happens to be honest, but lately it seems to be stronger." Mrs Faversham shrugged and watched Mrs B over the rim of her teacup.

"Well, you help people with your messages, don't you, dear? Just like Mr Endersleigh. Do you remember him?" Mrs B took a bite from her teacake.

"Yes, he was a funny man, so quick to jump and run when I warned him." Mrs Faversham drained the last of her tea.

"I am so very glad that we had this chance to talk, dear." Mrs B reached across the table and patted her hand. She watched Mrs Faversham leave the café, and paid the bill. Across the road, Will was waiting in the car with Arnold. "Well, I think we were absolutely correct. We must go ahead with the plan tonight."

"I will not be there in an official capacity." Arnold shook his head.

"Of course not, dear, you will be there as my nephew." Mrs B patted his hand and sat back in the seat as Will started the engine.

81.

Mrs B brings her own message

"It's nine twenty-five, dear." Will reached for Mrs B's hand.

"Yes indeed. We should get ourselves in position." Mrs B smiled across the car at him.

Will had parked down the road from Mrs Faversham's house. They walked slowly towards her front gate, Mrs B's arm tucked into Will's elbow. Arnold followed behind them.

"Here we are." Mrs B nodded to the house, where the curtains were closed, and only a glow in the windows suggested that anybody was at home. "Come along Arnold. It's time for your performance."

"I feel a little foolish." Arnold whispered to his aunt.

"You will feel worse than that if I am wrong." Mrs B snapped a smile at him.

"Fine." Arnold followed her around the side of the house.

"It has to be here." Mrs B pushed aside the bushes

"No. Well then, how?" She reached for the next shrub and pulled it sideways.

"Here." Will pointed to a ventilated brick just a foot above the earth around the base of the wall.

"Thank you, Will." She stood back and pointed to the brick. "Arnold. Here."

Arnold leaned towards the brick and checked his watch. The sound of steps on the pathway made them all turn their heads.

Will pointed towards the trees and larger shrubs and all three pushed themselves into the shadow of the trees. The grass was a little wet from the rain earlier in the evening, she could smell it.

The man who had been coming up the path leaned towards the ventilated brick and spoke, his voice soft and gentle. "Eileen, I have a message for you. Listen very carefully." He took a breath. "Mr Endersleigh needs your help. His father will die unless he resolves the problems. It is of the utmost importance that he does it tomorrow."

Arnold stood up a little straighter, and took a step forward. "You're under arrest Brian Ellis. On charges of blackmail and gaining pecuniary advantage by fraudulent means. I am sure that you are breaking a few other laws, but we will have to work that out as we go. You will be spending a good few years away, my old chum."

"What? You've got no proof of any of that." He tried to pull away, but Arnold had hold of his arm and led him away, paying no attention to his arguments.

"That's great news. Now that Mr Endersleigh and his father are safe, they will, I am sure, be happy to give evidence against Mrs Faversham's brother, Arnold will have no difficulty in making the case. You are a really rather wonderful detective." Will leaned down to kiss Mrs B.

"I'm glad we didn't have to send Mrs Faversham a fake message to prove a point. It was an unfair way to use her. I am certain that she does believe in what she does. Her brother just took advantage." She reached for Will's hand and they set off for the garden gate.

Light spilled from the front door when it opened. "What are you doing here?" Mrs Faversham was silhouetted against the light from her hallway.

"I wanted to thank you, and apologise. I know that you came to me with that message from Herbert in good faith, and I might have been a little brusque." Mrs B stepped into the light so that Mrs Faversham could see her clearly.

"He's happy for you. You're right, he's a kind man. He told me that you should wear the watch he gave you on your wedding day. You might need to know you're on time." Mrs Faversham shrugged. "Don't ask me to explain, but I think you've been lucky to find two decent men who love you. I've never found one." She laughed, and closed the door, leaving Mrs B and Will standing on the path listening to the laughter.

"Well, whatever next?" Mrs B felt Will's hand in the small of her back, and together they walked back down the road to his parked car.

82.

Mrs B has a reminder

"Well now. We are here. Clearly you are here too. This is perfect timing. Come along." Mrs Lennet and Barbara bustled into Mrs B's kitchen.

"Where are we going?" Mrs B seemed worried.

"Oh, we aren't going anywhere. We do have a great deal to do, though." Barbara smiled and held Mrs B's hands. "We only have a little under two weeks until the wedding in case you have forgotten, and we need to make you entirely perfect before that."

"I do not wish to be perfect, Barbara. Will is marrying me. He is wholly aware that I am no longer seventeen." Mrs B shook her head. "I am not going to undergo any sort of…..beautification process." Mrs B shook her head. "Now, would you ladies like a cup of tea?"

"I am ready for a cup, and this is not about beautification. It is about being relaxed and taken care of, feeling wonderful when you walk down the aisle. It has nothing to do with your looks." Mrs Lennet smiled gently. "Except we will be doing your hair and your nails. Perhaps shaving your legs and doing some basic skincare. That's all."

"Is it really less than two weeks?" Mrs B fetched the teapot and measured out the tea leaves. "That is a very short time."

"Yes, it is. But we still have time for tea." Barbara laughed.

"Nails you say?" Mrs B fetched cups and saucers.

"Yes, and hair." Mrs Lennet confirmed.

"Oh." Mrs B set the teapot on the table. "Do you imagine that Will would expect this to happen?"

"I have no idea what Will expects. However, I do know that we love you, and we want you to be as lovely as you are, we want to help you. It will be fun." Barbara reached across the table and held Mrs B's hand.

"Will it? I have to be honest. I find that hard to believe." Mrs B poured the tea and pushed cups across to her guests. "What do you mean by nails?"

Barbara opened her bag and pulled out three bottles of nail varnish, one was clear, the other two delicate shades of pink. "What do you think?"

"I think you have a good deal to teach me." Mrs B sipped her tea and smiled across at them. "But if I do not like it, I am not going to wear it to the wedding."

"That is entirely understood." Mrs Lennet raised her teacup in a toast, and the three of them clinked their cups together.

83.

Mrs B has a visitor

If Mrs B was feeling a little self-conscious, now that her nails were shaped and her hair had been skilfully cut and twisted into a chignon, she tried hard to control her feelings. The church waited for her, an oasis of calm and quiet.

Mrs Chambers peered out of the vestry. "Oh, Mrs B, what good timing. I was just clearing the last of the flowers from last week. I had a kind message from Mrs Lennet asking me to meet her for tea to talk about the flowers for your big day. Everyone is so excited." She wrapped the dead flowers in the newspaper she had spread out on the table. "The whole village is coming to celebrate with you." She smiled and hugged Mrs B. "I must hurry. I need to call in on Mrs Pendle. It was lovely to see you."

Mrs B sank into one of the pews. Her mind working carefully through the last few days.

"Mrs B?" She was startled by the voice.

"Reverend Chambers?" Mrs B turned in her seat.

"You were so far away. Can I help you, my

friend?" He sat down in the pew next to her.

"I am caught in a storm of everyone's good wishes. I confess, it is making me feel quite giddy and uncomfortable. Everyone has been so kind, helping with the wedding, but it seems it has almost come to the day, without my realising it. I am not sure how to do this." Mrs B swiped at a tear. "For heaven's sake, now I'm crying. This is ridiculous. I am a rational human being. Why am I behaving like this?"

"You are entirely rational. Marriage is an enormous commitment, and standing on the edge of the decision, even when you know entirely that it is the right one, is rightly a moment to take stock." He patted her hand. "I believe that this is a standard reaction to the approach of matrimony. Mrs Chambers locked herself in her bedroom and refused to come out for three days the week before we married." He laughed. "Perhaps she was right, but we have a good life and a wonderful family."

"I didn't feel this way when I married Herbert." She shook her head.

"Perhaps you should have." Reverend Chambers patted her shoulder and pushed himself up to his feet. "Will loves you, of that, I am sure. As certain as I am that you love him. I have never seen you happier. Yet you seem to wish to deny yourself that. Nerves are perfectly natural, but if there is something else that is worrying you, then tell me."

"You're right. Thank you. I have been behaving in the most ridiculous way." She smiled at the startled vicar and, having bowed her head to the altar, rushed from the church. "Thank you, Reverend."

The hill was as steep as it always was, but her steps were quick and light. She arrived at her garden gate to find that Mrs Endersleigh was waiting for her.

"Mrs Endersleigh. How lovely. I was about to have a cup of tea. Will you join me?" Mrs B opened the back door and led her guest into the kitchen.

"Mrs B. I wanted to thank you. My husband told me what happened. That man put us, and my father-in-law, an elderly frail man, in danger. It was unforgivable. Now that your nephew has the culprit in custody, and my husband and his father are safe and at home, I have come to settle my debt with you." She sat down at the table. "Thank you for bringing him home to me." She reached into her handbag and brought out a lace-edged handkerchief, which she used to blot her tears. "We have been married since I was seventeen. I suspect that we have grown used to each other, and are often irritated by the other's actions. I realised when he was missing how much I love him. In a way, it has been a fresh start for both of us." She pulled out an envelope and placed it on the table. "This is what I owe you, and a little more." She smiled. "A wedding gift, from one couple to another."

"How very kind, Mrs Endersleigh. I was quite nervous about the wedding, which is unusual for me. I am not given to flights of fancy or ungrounded worrying. Generally, I am almost entirely sensible." Mrs B pushed a cup of tea and a plate of biscuits towards Mrs Endersleigh. "It has been a most surprising few days."

"Yes, indeed, it has." Mrs Endersleigh took a biscuit from the plate and bit into it. "Oh my, these are delicious."

"Thank you. I'll be making some for the wedding. I hope you and Mr Endersleigh will be able to join us."

84.

Mrs B discovers some old traditions

"Good afternoon, Mrs B." Mrs Lennet opened the back door.

"Mrs Lennet? I am so sorry, did we have an arrangement to meet, have I forgotten something?" Mrs B poured the boiling water from the kettle into the teapot.

"No, not at all. I have popped in purely on the off chance that you would be free, and that you could make some time for me." Mrs Lennet sat at the kitchen table.

"At least we can have a cup of tea together." Mrs B put the cups and saucers on the table.

"Oh my, Mrs B. We have time for a cup of tea, then we have a party to get to." Mrs Lennet's face was lit with a smile. "It's a tradition. The women of the village want to wish you well."

"Oh, no no, no." Mrs B sat down at the table. "There will be none of that. I am not a young bride just out of pigtails. For heaven's sake."

"This is not about age. People in this village

love you. Let us celebrate with you." Mrs Lennet leaned across the table and took Mrs B's hands in her own. "Come on, it might even be fun." She laughed. Mrs B lifted an eyebrow and watched the laughter change the shape of Mrs Lennet's face.

"Fine. It seems I have little choice. Perhaps I should give in gracefully." Mrs B laughed. "Just please, can we keep it civilised?"

"I promise. Let's finish this cup of tea and then we are off to the church hall, and an afternoon with friends and happiness." Mrs Lennet raised her teacup from her saucer in a toast.

The church hall was decked out in bunting, that was usually used for parties in the village. "Well, it seems that someone has been busy here!" Mrs B allowed herself to be shepherded into the hall.

"Surprise!" The shout filled the hall.

"Oh my. Well, how lovely to see you all." Mrs B reached out and hugged Mrs Appleby. "You are looking very well. How nice." Each step forward, she met another friend, and received another hug. "I am a little overwhelmed."

"We have some things to do." Mrs Caldecot led her to the table at the back of the hall, where Mrs Pendle was sitting.

"You should be resting." Mrs B shook her head.

"I am. Mrs Lennet even collected me in her car,

and will take me home when we are all finished here." She patted the chair next to her. "They won't let you go home until we make the flower garlands."

Mrs B shook her head, but she joined Mrs Pendle, and the other ladies took their seats. Each lady had a small ring, as wide as their spread fingers in front of them, a roll of white cotton and a pile of flowers. "I am too old for all this." Mrs B shook her head.

"Nonsense. This is a wonderful ancient tradition. We are part of history, just by doing this today." Mrs Pendle patted her hand.

Each woman took a flower and the ring and twined the stem around the ring, securing it with the cotton, then they added the next flower, and the next.

"You know that this is a pagan ritual, a fertility rite. I am beyond an age when I will be likely to conceive, and I am unsure if I am completely comfortable with the pagan side of it." Mrs B kept her voice low, but she knew that Mrs Pendle had heard her, and was laughing quietly.

"Yes, probably the root of the ritual is pagan. The original idea might have been fertility, but why not take it as a wish for a happy marriage, or just a show of support?" Mrs Pendle patted Mrs B's hand. "Everyone gets nervous before they get married. It's normal. This is a way of telling you that we're all standing with you." She pointed to Mrs B's flowers. "You have some catching up to do."

"Yes, I do." Mrs B did not pick up the flowers. She looked around the room. Each woman sat at the table, chatting and enjoying the time with friends, but they were all here to wish her well. She felt a tear spring to her eye and brushed away the feeling with it. "I owe all of you an apology, and a good deal more than a cup of tea and biscuit. I have been so busy, perhaps I have had less time for my friends." Mrs B reached for the flowers and began making the garland. "A timely reminder, ladies. Thank you." Her comment was met with smiles from around the village hall.

85.

Mrs B receives a sombre visit

"Mrs B? Oh, my goodness, I don't know who else I can go to. Please help me." Pamela burst into the kitchen.

"Pamela, whatever has happened?" Mrs B reached for her and wrapped her arms around her. It only took a glance to see that she had been crying, her eyes were red and her pale skin blotchy.

"My grandma died yesterday." She slumped into one of the chairs at the table.

"Oh, my love. You poor thing. I am so sorry. It must have been very difficult for you." Mrs B reached for Pamela's hands. "We should go to the prison and tell your mother, perhaps."

"No, I already did that." Her head sank down onto her crossed arms, her shoulders heaving with the sobs.

"Oh, darling Pamela." Mrs B stroked the poor girl's back. "I'll make a cup of tea and we'll work out what needs to be done." She filled the kettle and put it onto the stove, listening to the soft, exhausted sounds of Pamela's sobs. When the whistle came, Pamela was starting to wipe her face, and the tears had slowed. "Here we are. Have a cup of tea. Tell me what happened."

"I went to see her. I had to wait and wait. Now that I'm back, I wish I had asked you to come with me. Instead, I was all alone in that cold room. But they never told me. They thought that I knew, because I was there, I suppose. Oh, Mrs B. I have spent so many years being angry with my family. I've been a complete fool." She wiped her face.

"This is becoming a little confusing, Pamela. Please start at the beginning and tell me what happened?" Mrs B sat opposite her and held her hand.

"Grandma had been getting more and more tired. We knew she had very little time left. I sat with her for three days and nights, and gradually she slipped away. It was sad, but not entirely unexpected. I just sat with her and cried until the morning. You were right. The first thing I thought of was that I should go and tell my mother. I mean, she had lost her mother after they had just made it up. It was the most cruel thing to have happened." She took a sip of her tea. "Oh, for heaven's sake, why would this happen?"

"It's so sad that your grandma passed away. But it must have been a comfort to her to know that you were with her at the end. Perhaps that was why she was so peaceful and she could slip away. What you have done for her is a wonderful gift." Mrs B felt the grip of her fingers tighten.

"That's so kind. I just thought it was the right thing to do, but then I drove to the prison. I explained to the guards who I was, and they let me in and put me in a room to wait." She took a deep breath.

"Where was your husband? It would have been better if Gregory had gone with you, surely?" Mrs B felt her face filling with disapproval and concentrated on keeping her expression neutral.

"He had a full day of appointments. It would have been unfair to pull him away. I thought I would be able to manage. In fact, it might be because I had missed out on so much sleep, but I felt quite able to do whatever was needed." She rolled her lips over each other.

"Oh, my dear." Mrs B pulled the young girl into her arms and held her. "Let's not worry about what happened for a minute. Life will go on. It seems impossible that it could right now, but you will see. There will come a time when you will remember how much love your grandma gave you and not the pain of living without her."

"I knew you would understand, Mrs B." Pamela took a sip from her tea. "Thank you."

86.

Mrs B finds out more

"So, what was it that you heard at the prison that upset you so much?" Mrs B held Pamela's hand in both of hers.

"Nothing. Absolutely nothing. Nobody told me a thing. In fact, strangely, it was as though they wanted to avoid talking to me. They took me up through the prison, into the hospital part. I could hear people in the rooms they passed. Some of them were crying, or moaning and there was a smell, like dirt and something I didn't recognise." Pamela ran her hand through her hair. "She was in a bed at the far end of the room, just lying there. I sat in a chair and held her hand. Before I even got to her, I was telling her, what had happened, why I had missed the visit the day before. It was spilling out of me, like I couldn't hold it in." She swallowed hard. "I was too late. She was gone too. After all the arguing and fighting, I have lost both of them." Her voice caught on the words.

"Oh Pamela. I am so sorry. That is truly heartbreaking." Mrs B stroked Pamela's hair. "You poor girl."

"I don't know what to do." Pamela wiped her eyes. "Without them, I have no way to go forward."

"Oh, but you do. You have the strength that they gave you and the lessons that they taught you. They are a part of you. Now it's time for you to carry on and make them even more proud of you than they were." Mrs B pulled her chair around so that she was next to Pamela.

"You always know the right thing to say, Mrs B." Pamela patted Mrs B's hand.

"Well now, you have had a very difficult few days, haven't you? We will need to talk to your husband and get some advice about the practicalities, but in the meantime, I think you have had quite enough for now." She shepherded Pamela through to the living room, where she helped her onto the sofa, and pulled a soft blanket over her. "Sleep for a little while and I will be right here when you wake up." Mrs B leaned down and kissed her gently on the cheek. "Emotion is exhausting. So, take a nap." She listened to Pamela's regular breathing and stepped away from her. With great care, she pulled the door almost closed, and went back to her kitchen, where she said a silent prayer for both of the very strong women who had been so difficult, annoying and filled with fight and anger. She wished them well on the next part of their journey and thanked them for the love they had both given to Pamela.

87.

Mrs B shares her flowers

"My dear, it makes absolute sense." Mrs B rested her hand on Pamela's shoulder. "In fact, the more I think about it, the better an idea I think it is."

"She's right. There is no sense in wasting a beautifully decorated church. It would be our very great honour to share the church with your mother and grandmother." Will sat down at the table with them.

"But it seems such an intrusion into your wedding. The flowers are there for you and Will." Pamela was definitely looking better than she had done. A good night's sleep and the resilience of youth had banished the dark circles under her eyes and put a little colour back into her cheeks.

"No intrusion at all." Mrs B smiled and caught Will's gentle smile over Pamela's shoulder.

"Reverend Chambers says that it's possible, and the prison telephoned my husband to agree that my mother's body can be released. In fact, he has been very helpful with all of this. I'll ask him to arrange for my mother and my grandmother to be brought to the church, if you're absolutely certain." Pamela sat up straighter. "I have told everyone that I can think of, and you know how these things are. The news will spread. One thing that I do not want is a church full of every criminal in a hundred-mile radius. Maybe a quick funeral is better, all things considered." She squeezed Mrs B's fingers tightly, then checked her wristwatch. "Thank you."

"No thanks needed. Now, go home and get ready." Mrs B stood up. "We will walk down to the surgery and meet you both there, so that we can go down to the church together."

"Thank you, Mrs B. Thank you, Will. We'll be ready." She let herself out of the back door and left Mrs B and Will to get changed in to their dark sombre suits, to bid farewell to two women who had caused great trouble, in order to protect Pamela.

The sun broke through the clouds just as the two hearses arrived at the church. Respectful undertakers carried the matching coffins into the church, and stood back, making shallow bows to the altar before walking through the church, eyes focused on the front door, where Pamela waited with Mrs B and Will standing either side of her. Her husband arrived just in time to walk in with them, and Mrs B restrained her thoughts. This was no time to be disapproving of the man who loved young

Pamela.

Mr Bisley had saved them a seat at the front of the church. He wrapped his daughter in a hug, struggling to stay strong, while his eyes swam with tears.

Mrs B spotted Mr McKinley across the other side of the church and nodded her greeting. There were a good many people in the church that she had never seen before, and a familiar face felt like a blessing.

The Reverend Chambers called for her attention, along with the rest of the congregation. He told them a little about the two women they had come to say goodbye to. He talked about the fierce love they had for their families and the pride they had in Pamela. Mrs B listened to the words and breathed in the scent of flowers which had been placed in the church for her wedding and now were dressing the church for a double funeral.

The stories and the gentle tone washed over her, and she felt the solidness of Will sitting next to her. Very soon, it was all over, and time for the two coffins to be moved for the last time.

Later, when everyone was gone, and Mr McKinley had told her that he was looking forward to the wedding the next day. When Pamela had hugged her family and shaken hands with more people than she wanted to remember, they went home, leaving Mr Bisley at the church with a hug. Pamela fell asleep before they had time to even think about making her a cup of tea, exhausted by the emotion and the strain. Her husband, so competent as a doctor, was worried about his wife, and his jitters made Mrs B feel more kindly towards him.

"She will be absolutely fine Gregory. The best thing for her is to sleep, and recover from the last few days." Mrs B patted his arm. "She is going to make a very good doctor's wife."

Will took her hand as they left the young couple behind and walked up the hill. "Are you still nervous about the wedding?" He watched her face.

"No. Yes. A little. Are you?" She stopped walking and turned to look at him.

"I'm terrified. What if I say the wrong thing, or do something stupid?" He took a deep breath.

"You certainly would not do either of those things. We will be perfectly fine." Mrs B smoothed her hand across the lapel of his jacket.

"So why are you nervous?" He smiled.

"I'm really not anymore. I am certain that this is the right thing to do, and I am over the nerves. Or at least, most of them." She laughed, and he laughed with her and took her hand.

88.

Mrs B makes her peace

"I need to go and pick up something for tomorrow. Are you alright?" Will wrapped his arms around Mrs B.

"Yes, I think I will go for a walk. It feels like time for some quiet reflection." She reached up to kiss his cheek and watched him drive away.

The lanes were filled with memories. Her childhood, and later during the war, when she had been married, and then widowed. Outside the church, she stopped and took a look at the two new graves. They were alone together, now that all the mourners had gone. It seemed fitting. Perhaps that was all they had ever really needed.

The door to the church stood open, and she went inside, bowing her head to the altar, and finding a seat at the back. She said a silent prayer for the two women in the graveyard, and for Pamela who had been left behind.

The smell of burning incense interrupted her thoughts, and she opened her eyes. "Reverend Chambers? Are you quite well?"

"Oh! Mrs B?" He seemed startled. "I was just, well, that is to say, I am making certain that…" He slumped into the pew in front of her. "I wanted to make sure, and I know that you will think me a silly old fool, but today you did a very generous thing for young Pamela, and I am certain that she should be most grateful to you. But I did not grow up in a peaceful village like this one. I spent my formative years in the backstreets of a city where crime and mean spirits were more common than kindness. I saw that in the faces of the men in the church today." He shook his head. "I got it into my head to clean the church from their unkindness before your wedding tomorrow. Good grief. Now that I have said it out loud, it sounds even sillier than it did in my head."

"You are swinging that incense around to cleanse the church? Oh, my dear friend, I think that is one of the kindest things that I have ever heard of." She smiled and took his hands in hers.

"Now you think I am not thinking straight." He shrugged. "I suspect that is nothing new." He laughed.

"I have always believed that the best way to freshen a building is to open the doors and let the fresh air in." Mrs B smiled.

"What a very good idea." He smiled. "Let's do exactly that."

He walked to the back of the church and pushed both doors open. A breeze filled the building and Mrs B stood by the Reverend Chambers as the scent of the incense cleared to be replaced by the soft fragrance of fresh flowers.

"Are you ready for tomorrow, Mrs B?" He turned to smile at her.

"I am. In fact, I am looking forward to it." She tipped her head to one side and realised that it was the truth. She had put her wedding out of her mind while she concentrated on other things. Almost any other thing. But that was over.

"Well, isn't that the very best timing, because I do believe that the church is now ready for you." He turned back towards the altar and she took another look, turning slowly through a circle to take in the whole building.

"You're right. It has never looked more beautiful. Thank you so much for worrying about it, but I think this is absolutely perfect as it is." She smiled up at him.

"My dear friend. I am so pleased that you and Will have found each other. Tomorrow, it will be my great pleasure to help you to seal your vows to each other." He patted her hand and carried the incense back towards the altar.

"Thank you, Reverend Chambers. I will see you tomorrow." Mrs B waved from the door.

"Yes, indeed. Make sure that you are on time. Your groom and I will be waiting." He chuckled to himself and waved back.

89.

Mrs B's day begins

The knock on the door surprised Mrs B. Marmalade was a little put out that he had to be placed onto the floor when he had been perfectly content to sit on her knee and sleep.

"Mrs B? I am so sorry to disturb you so early, but I am in quite a pickle. It seems that I have lost something that is really absolutely essential for today. I wonder if Little Mellington's finest detective might help me to find it." Mrs Lennet bustled her way into the kitchen.

"I am so sorry, Mrs Lennet. What is it that you have lost?" Mrs B wondered what could possibly be so important on a day which was supposed to be her wedding day, but Mrs Lennet was a dear friend, and she had no wish to upset her any further. Mrs B checked her watch. It was just a little before ten and she had to be at the church at three, so she had an hour, or maybe two, to give to her dear friend.

"I must admit, I am quite distracted, my dear Mrs B. There is no time to lose, I am afraid. I know that you have a busy day ahead, but if you would just help me with this, I would be so absolutely in your debt." Mrs Lennet waited only long enough for Mrs B to feed the cat, before bustling her out to the car, and directing the driver to take them both to the Manor with all possible speed.

When Mrs B stepped out of the car, she wondered if the slightly dizzy feeling she had was caused by the speed of the car, or the constant chattering from Mrs Lennet.

"Do come in, Mrs B. Mrs Lennet led the way. I last saw it up here, so I suspect that is the best place to find it." Mrs B followed her friend up the stairs and into a part of the house she had not seen before. A long room where a small crowd of women waited. She spotted Barbara, Mrs Pendle, who she was glad to see was sitting down, Mrs Appleby and Mrs Chambers. There were two other women she did not recognise.

"Whatever is this about, Mrs Lennet? What is it that you have lost?" Mrs B's brows furrowed.

"Dear friend. We are here to see you off to your wedding. See, here is your gown, your hairdresser, and this lovely lady will give you a manicure. Your shoes are waiting. Everything is prepared. All these ladies are here to send you to your wedding with their love. What we had lost was the bride, and now we have found her." Mrs Lennet smiled widely, pleased by her kind and gentle deception, and Mrs B allowed herself to be led to a chair, and to be given a cup of tea and an iced bun.

90.

Mrs B is ready

"Have you finished your tea?" The hairdresser passed Mrs B a warm robe and led her to a small dressing room off the main area. "Pop that on, and we can start getting your hair done. I know everyone is very excited." She smiled. It was professional but also there was warmth there. Mrs B nodded and went into the room. She quickly undressed down to her slip and pushed her arms into the robe. She found a pair of comfortable slippers waiting for her, too.

"Here she is." Mrs Appleby met her by the door. "This is the most exciting thing. None of us could believe that Mrs Lennet had planned all of this. It's going to be a wonderful day."

"I found slippers in there. It's all very strange." Mrs B raised her eyebrow at Mrs Appleby.

The hairdresser set to work, spraying Mrs B's hair and putting in rollers. A lady in a blue sweater sat next to Mrs B and went to work on her nails. "So, today is your big day? It's so exciting. Mrs Lennet is a wonderful person. She must think the world of you." The girl smiled and bent her head, going back to work and leaving Mrs B with beautifully shaped nails and hands smoothed with cream that smelled like a spring garden and made her smile. She stopped smiling when the girl knelt to shape her toenails. She laughed out loud as the tickles ran around her feet. When the girl had finished, and her feet smelled as wonderful as her hands, she wrapped a towel around them and left her with a gentle pat on her knee. "Enjoy your day."

The hairdresser returned just a few minutes later and carefully took out the rollers. "Well, now, here we are. I am going to do your hair as we did before when we tried it all out, but I'll add a few little extras and hope that you like it." She laughed and rested her hand on Mrs B's shoulder. "You really don't need to look so frightened."

Mrs B closed her eyes and wondered whatever would come next. "Do you think this is necessary? I mean, he wanted to marry me when I had ragged nails and my own hair pulled back out of the way. Should I not go to the church as myself? This feels a little as though I'm pretending."

"You are yourself. From what Mrs Lennet says, he adores you. All I'm doing is giving you the confidence to walk into the church and feel perfect." She pushed a pin into Mrs B's hair.

"Very well. You seem to know more about this than I do. I shall bow to your expertise in this matter." Mrs B smiled into the mirror in front of her and the hairdresser smiled back.

"I wonder, this is really cheeky on your big day, but Mrs Lennet tells me that you are a detective. Could I come to see you once you get back from your honeymoon?" She smoothed Mrs B's hair and slid another pin into the chignon.

"You need an investigator?" Mrs B sat up a little straighter.

"I think so. But there is no rush. I will visit you once you get home and all the kerfuffle has died down, if that is alright?" She patted Mrs B on the shoulder. "That's all done. You look really lovely. Congratulations, Mrs B. I will see you soon." She leaned in for a gentle hug and she was gone.

"Mrs B? We really do not have long now. Let's get you dressed. Oh my, your hair is wonderful. Karen has done a very good job." Mrs Lennet stood back and watched. "I've hung up your clothes in the room where you changed before."

In the small changing room Mrs B found not only the dress and jacket that Mrs Lennet had bought when they had gone shopping together but also silk stockings, underwear the like of which she had never seen and her shoes. With shaking fingers, she dressed and slipped her feet into the shoes that waited for her. When she turned and looked into the enormous mirror, her breath caught in her throat. "Oh my. I am fairly certain that I do not even look like me a little." She stepped closer. "Maybe a more polished version of me? I wonder if Will would think me foolish?" She smiled at herself. "I expect we shall find out."

91.

Mrs B and her entourage

For a moment, just one, she was worried to open the door. If she turned the handle, she would change everything. Perhaps she would lose a part of herself. Her hand rested on the door handle and she imagined Will, laughing at her for being an idiot. It helped.

"Oh now, here comes the bride. You look wonderful." Mrs Lennet gently squeezed Mrs B's shoulders. She checked her watch. "We need to go or your groom will be getting nervous."

Mrs B realised that they were alone in the room. "Where did the other ladies go?"

"My driver has been ferrying them to the church while you were dressing. I will go on next, along with my family and the lovely Barbara. Your nephew and another young man are waiting for you downstairs. I am so very happy for you." Mrs Lennet opened the door to the upstairs hallway and led her to the top of the stairs. "Are you ready?"

"I am a little nervous. Am I making the right

decision?" Mrs B rested her hand on the banister rail.

"Do you love him?" Mrs Lennet turned to face her.

"Yes, I do, and he loves me. Is that enough?" Mrs B met her friend's smile.

"You also have a profession in common, and a business to run together. Love is a good starting point. The pair of you have proved you have that, and trust and, more than that, you are friends. I think you will be just fine." Mrs Lennet patted her friend's hand.

"Thank you. For everything today, and for being my friend." Mrs B squared her shoulders and started down the stairs. Arnold stood on the bottom step and turned when he heard her footsteps.

"Auntie! My goodness, you look wonderful. We thought perhaps you might be nervous." He reached down to kiss her cheek.

"Perish the thought." She caught a look from Mrs Lennet and smiled. Barbara hugged her and waved as she left with Mr and Mrs Lennet.

"Mrs B? What have they done to you? You look like a film star." Tommy McKinley stepped out of the shadows. He wrapped an arm around her shoulders. "Better than when you borrowed my trousers, that's for sure!"

"Tommy! Yes, that was an adventure. I feel a little over dressed. Is Maisie alright? And the baby?" Mrs B smiled.

"They are both positively in the pink, and I think your car has arrived. You will see them at the church. Arnold will do a wonderful job of giving you away, but I begged and pleaded to be allowed to see you for a minute before you go, just to wish you luck and to say thank you." He leaned down and kissed her cheek. "Best friend I ever had."

"Heavens. What a lovely thing to say, Tommy. I am touched." Mrs B reached up and rested her hand on his shoulder.

"Come on Auntie. Tommy's right. We had better go." Arnold stood near to the door, shifting his weight from one foot to another.

"May I say, you look absolutely wonderful, ma'am?" Mrs Lennet's driver held the door open and waited while she climbed inside. Once Arnold and Tommy had joined her in the back, he set off at a sedate pace towards the church.

"Thank you, Mr Boskins." Mrs B settled back in the seat.

"You remembered my name ma'am?" Mrs Lennet's driver sat up a little straighter.

"Mrs B rarely forgets anything, Mr Boskins." Tommy laughed.

"Will's ever so nervous." Arnold laughed. "I told

him you'd be totally calm."

92.

Mrs B makes a promise

When she looked inside the church, Mrs B could just see the Reverend Chambers, and the sight of her old friend calmed whatever nerves were still worrying her. Mrs Lennet placed her bouquet in her hands and waited for a moment, before kissing her cheek and slipping into the church. Tommy slipped inside and signalled to Mr Phelps at the organ. He nodded and finished the piece that he had been playing. She checked her watch. Exactly three o'clock, on time, as promised.

A smile spread across Mrs B's face when she heard the song roll out of the church, a wave of wonder, as the notes soared to the beamed ceiling, stirring the dust motes and seeming to pull the congregation to their feet. Maisie was singing. Ave Maria swelled through the church and Arnold offered his aunt his elbow. She nodded. She was ready.

Her first step onto the wide flagstones took her into the space that had always been her safe place. The end of each pew was decorated with a circular flower garland. Each one made by one of the ladies of the village. Every bloom and thread gave her the courage to step forwards.

"I'm very proud of you Auntie." Arnold matched his pace to hers. She turned to look at him.

"I'm proud of you too, Arnold. Thank you for agreeing to do this." She smiled up at him. "You have been a joy and a comfort to me since the day your mother brought you into the world."

They stopped a few steps from the altar. "This is my stop." Arnold smiled.

"I suspect I am on my own now." Mrs B nodded.

"Not for long." Arnold nodded towards Will who waited at the altar for her. Mrs B smiled and stepped forward.

"Hello." She turned to Will and smiled.

"Well, I am so glad to see you." Will raised his eyebrow. "I thought perhaps you changed your mind."

"Perish the thought, Will." She smiled and reached for his hand.

The last notes of Ave Maria died away, and the congregation sat down. The Reverend Chambers cleared his throat, smiled at Mrs B and at Will, and he began.

"Dearly beloved, we are gathered here today, to join this man and this woman in holy matrimony." The Reverend Chambers smiled out across the church.

Later, when she thought about it, Mrs B would not be able to recall what was said word for word, but she knew how she felt when she promised. She felt as though she had come home.

When they stepped out into the sunshine, Will pulled her close and she felt the warmth of him through his shirt, she knew that he felt the same. "Very apt, the choice of music. Ave Maria. Hail Mary, and there you were, my very own darling wife, Mary Hunton. I do love you, Mrs Hunton."

"I love you too, my darling husband." She laughed when his eyebrows shot up, and she rested her hand against his chest. This very private moment between the two of them, before their guests joined them, before there was beer or sherry, or kisses from the family. It was, as it would be from that moment on, just Will and Mary. Exactly as it should be.

93.

Mrs B or ?

"You look wonderful. I don't know what else I will remember about today, but I will carry a picture in my head of the way you look today for the rest of my life." He smiled and squeezed her hand.

"I cannot believe how many people are here today. They came out for us, Will." She squeezed his hand, too.

"Mrs B?" Mrs Lennet smiled widely. "No, sorry, Mrs H."

"I think a good many people are going to struggle to remember that. In fact, I think I may find it difficult." Mrs B smiled.

"Oh, I meant to talk to you about that. What are we going to do about a new name for you?" He tipped his head to one side. "I don't want to change you. I just want you and me to be together. How about a compromise?" She turned to see what he had in mind. "You can be Mrs B, or Mrs H, or we can hyphenate it. Just be mine."

"I am yours, and you're mine." She lifted her

left hand and waggled her ring finger at him. "Always. Mrs Lennet reminded me earlier that we love each other, but more than that, we have a shared profession and a business, and we are friends. Oh, I forgot, I think we have a new case. Once we get back from honeymoon."

"I'll look forward to that." He laughed.

"To the new case?" Mrs B's brow creased.

"To the honeymoon! Also, to the sausage rolls and perhaps a little dancing. A beer or two, and a life together to look forward to. Oh, and yes, the new case that you forgot to tell me about." He took her hand. "Now, we have guests to thank, and sausage rolls to eat. What time is the food going to be ready?"

Mrs B checked her watch. "Well, now, that is the strangest thing. My watch has stopped at exactly three o'clock. It has never done that before. Perhaps I should take it to be repaired." She shook her head. "Not really something to worry about today."

"Strangely, today is exactly the day to worry about it." He reached into his pocket and pulled out a box. "Mrs Faversham came to see me. She told me that you would need a new watch." He shrugged and opened the box for her.

"Thank you, Will. That is very strange. It stopped at three, when I arrived at the church. This is beautiful. We are right on time, for the wedding, and for the food, if you're hungry." She smiled and squeezed his arm.

"Perfect. Let's eat." He wrapped an arm around her shoulders. "I was too nervous for breakfast."

"Yes, I think that sounds like a very good start to our life together." Mrs B reached up and kissed him.

The sounds of a small band reached them from across the village green. Friends greeted them with congratulations, but honestly, though they smiled and thanked them, the only important thing was the two of them.

In the centre of the village green, Will wrapped his arms around her and they danced to the band. In all the world, she thought, there was nowhere that she would rather be.

94.

By the church gate, in the small shadow provided by the yew tree which had grown there since before anyone in the village could remember, Mrs Faversham watched the newly married couple. An indulgent smile on her lips.

"Are you alright Herbert?" Her smile was gentle.

"Yes. I am. She looks very happy and that was all that I wanted to see. She has been on her own for far too long. My time with her is over. It ended when she arrived at the church. Her time with Will starts now. I think they will be very well suited. I can rest now, and leave her to his care." He nodded to himself. "Thank you, Mrs Faversham for passing on my messages, and helping me to come and see her today." He turned his hat through a circle in his hands, holding the brim.

"It has been my pleasure. She's a special lady." Mrs Faversham leaned her weight against the gate and watched the dancers.

"Yes, she is." He turned back to watch the dancers. "Good luck, Mary." He held the hat in one hand and positioned it on his head. He smiled and walked away down the lane, up the hill and around the corner.

"Mrs Faversham? I am so glad that you were able to come. I thought it was you. Will has gone in search of sausage rolls." Mrs B, dressed in her bridal best reached for Mrs Faversham's hands. "Come and have a glass of sherry, something to eat?"

"I would not have missed it for the world. I wish you and your husband every happiness." Mrs Faversham pulled her into a hug. "Thank you for inviting me. Yes, I would very much enjoy a glass of sherry and a sausage roll."

"Come along with me then. We will have to hurry or they will all be gone. My husband is very hungry, and he does enjoy a sausage roll." Mrs B laughed and linked her arm through Mrs Faversham's. Together they walked towards the village hall and the promise of food, drink and a bright future.

Printed in Great Britain
by Amazon